ELEVATION OF MANA

✧ BOOK 4 ✧

ELEVATION OF MANA

BOOK 4

WANDERING AGENT

Podium

Cover design by Yanhong Lu

ISBN: 979-8-3470-4445-0

Published in 2026 by Podium Publishing
www.podiumentertainment.com

ELEVATION OF MANA

✧ BOOK 4 ✧

CHAPTER 1

WAKE UP

I was fast asleep when the blow came, so hard to the stomach that I shot awake, the air knocked out of me.

"OOF!" I grunted as I was thrust into consciousness.

"Wake up, Daddy!" came a high pitched, pleading call.

"Adia, Daddy needs to sleep," I grumbled, trying to rub my eyes.

"NOOOO, the sun's up!" she pried, squirming up beside me in the bed.

"All right, if the sun's up," I said, chuckling.

I'd only gone to bed a couple hours ago, but it was clear that my daughter had other ideas about me sleeping, and I was weak when it came to her. So I sat up, pulling her beside me.

"I brought you breakfast," she said, pointing to a small piece of fruit beside the bed. It was nowhere near enough for a meal, but she was four, so what could I really expect?

"Why thank you," I said, taking up the snack and munching on it. "Where's your mother?"

She shrugged, putting on the most innocent face she could, and I wasn't buying it one bit. For all that I loved Adia, I knew she was seldom alone. That may have been frowned upon by some, but I was now a major player in the city, and I didn't want anyone targeting my child. Mostly, I didn't like violence and would hate to have to explain to the other members of the council why I'd turned someone into a pink stain.

"Her mother," came a response from the hallway, "is looking for her wandering child."

Isha appeared in the door, looking none too thrilled.

"Come join us, dear," I said, offering the remains of the fruit. "We're having breakfast."

"I'll pass," she said, and then turned to Adia. "Didn't I tell you to let your father sleep?"

"He's been sleeping all morning," Adia whined.

"It's fine, love. I needed to get up anyway."

"Still," Isha said, joining us on the bed. "Justin, what's that?"

She carefully lifted her hand to my scalp, taking a few hairs in hand, eyes focused on one of them in particular. As the strands moved through her fingers I saw what she was talking about. Standing out in the light against the other hairs was one in particular, pale and shining white.

"Has it really been that long?" I asked, looking at it.

"You'll have to make an announcement," she said, releasing the hair. "And yes, it has."

I gave each of the two most important women in my life a quick kiss, one on the forehead and the other the lips, before rising in earnest.

"Looks like I actually do need to get up. Daddy's got to work now, but I'll be back for lunch, okay?" I said.

"Okay," Adia said with a small pout.

This was unexpected, odd because I was just a bit too young. At only eighty I'd be one of the youngest elders in history, but with the turning of my hair there was no denying it had come. Among family and friends there would be celebrations. Among detractors, grumbling. For now, the final objection to my place on the city's ruling council was gone.

My bedroom faded behind me as I began to move through the house, more like a mini-fortress or complex now. It wasn't modern, but it wasn't what I'd grown up in either. I'd had time, time and the mind to practice, to build, to hone skills, and teach them to others. Fabrics had replaced much of the furs, and spring beds replaced the piles of rushes we'd slept on for so long. There was even proper furniture and lighting, almost all the modern amenities I knew before were now at my fingertips, but not just through technology, but magic as well.

Not everyone had these things yet. Many villages remained almost completely unchanged from where they had been when I'd been born, but the city was changing rapidly. New streets, plumbing, drainage, materials, all moved outward from my home, all bringing society upward. Not everyone liked it—with old folks complaining about this and that—but enough did, and they loved it.

As I made my way down a staircase into the work areas of the complex, a girl at a shining desk stood and turned. "Good morning sir," she intoned.

"Good morning, please summon Chien to my workshop. I've a need to speak with him urgently."

She nodded and turned to a series of speaking tubes and levers mounted on the wall. I'd not managed to remake something like telephones yet, at least not on a level I would share, but these were manageable—signals to people all over the sprawling estate to communicate as needed. It was slow, but he'd get the message before too long.

Leaving her, I headed to my own space. No longer was it blocked by large slabs of stone, but proper doors with complex locks powered by magic and codes. Making something that could store magic as a usable energy was still beyond me, but I was getting closer. A small jolt into it and a few punched numbers on a little keypad, and it clicked open, letting me through.

Inside I went to my desk and sat, waiting. I hadn't been this nervous in some time, not since Adia's birth. That alone had been something that had nearly killed me.

Isha and I had tried for a child for so long and had so many issues. I didn't know if it was something about my being from another world, or something else about one of us, but it hadn't been easy. We'd consulted experts, tried again and again. She'd had miscarriages, a pair of stillborns, and failure after failure. She'd blamed herself, but I was fairly sure it was me.

Healers hadn't been able to tell us anything. Many seemed unconcerned, saying that sometimes it was like that, some people just had a hard time having children, that it would come with time. Others tried herbs and poultices. I bemoaned the fact that I'd never gotten proper medical training, trying to dig through my memories and failing repeatedly. We'd both suffered, until finally Adia had been born, a light for both of us, a sign of hope for our family.

Adia wasn't, so far as I could tell, like me and from another world. No, instead she was a normal, happy child. The girl was a bit of a handful some days, but others she was practically an angel. Naming her after my mother had been fortunate too, because though they were slight, there were signs that she had magic too. Her aura flared sometimes when she got bumps and bruises, and when it did, they healed. Perhaps it hadn't manifested fully yet, but soon it would, and she'd need training then.

"Hey, boss, you there?" Chien asked, waving a hand in front of my face.

"Oh, sorry, didn't even see you come in." I flushed as I turned toward one of my oldest friends.

"You really need to get more sleep," he chided, getting me to laugh.

"Soon, but first." I pulled the lock of hair forward showing him the pale strand.

"Finally! Took you long enough."

"I'm quite early to it," I scoffed.

"Nah, you were born old, boss, old and childish all at once."

CHAPTER 2

ANNOUNCEMENT PLANS

"I'm glad you're taking this so seriously," I said to my smiling assistant.

"As are you," he scoffed, and I had to laugh.

"Fair, but things will change."

"For the better."

"I agree, but we still need to be prepared," I informed him, trying to impress that others would now react to both of us differently.

"I prepared years ago, didn't you?" he answered flippantly.

"What?"

"Mind waiting here for a bit?" Chien asked.

"Sure . . ."

He ran off, and based on the direction he took off from, he was headed to his own workshop, but I didn't pry. I had my private spaces, and he had his. That had been an important thing for me, making sure those who worked with me felt respected. After all, I'd been in poor conditions before, and even an awful job or two back on Earth, so I knew the kind of resentment that could breed.

No, Chien had privacy. Even if he was within my compound, I always tried to give him his space. With how long we lived, that wasn't just decency either, but self-interest. Making an enemy of someone who could live for centuries was seldom worth it, and Chien was a friend, a rare thing for elders or ancients to maintain. I wanted him to remain a friend, and so if there was something within reason he wanted, I gave it to him.

While he was gone, I turned to look at my longtime project sitting in the corner of my room. My first attempts at a magical computer had been . . . a mess. Getting the proper amount of power to go through it without overloading the structure had been nigh impossible unless I managed it myself. Those early attempts had still been useful, in some ways. They could do calculations quickly, but with having to almost manually manage things, they were very limited in use.

The newer models had other crystals built into them though, tiny bits of physical property magic that would allow them to reach out into the world. I'd not solved all the problems yet, but we were making real progress. My issue was still getting them to interface with people properly, but that would come with time. That was my best guess at how to solve the power management issue.

Before I could get up and keep playing, though, Chien returned, a long box in hand.

"What do you have there?" I asked.

"Something I made for you," he said, chuckling.

"Should I be worried?"

"I wouldn't be."

He opened the box, something that on its own would've been impressive many years ago, but now was becoming more and more common, and pulled forth a robe. The fabric was light and fine, colored a deep blue, with small, hardly noticeable designs worked along the hems in black and white. With it were several pieces of jewelry, bracelets, and beads.

"Where in the world did you get that?" I asked, looking over the piece.

Cloth was gaining in popularity as things went on, but most of it wasn't anywhere near this quality. People were still learning fibers, methods, and tricks of the trade. Soon, such a robe might be something that could be bought, but I'd never seen such a piece for sale before.

"You remember Ida?" he asked, as if I couldn't remember literally everything.

"The slave girl Atal gave me? Yes, but I haven't seen her in ages."

"She's gone and joined a little group to the north. They've taken to cloth like birds to the sky. So, a few years back I sent her a request, for when this day came. This was the best they could make then, perhaps they could make something better now, but . . ."

"No, that's perfect," I said with a smile. Ida had been one of the first to take up making cloth, and to wear something she'd made would be an honor. After all, seeing the progress of those my life has touched was beautiful to me. "And the jewelry?"

"Oh, those are from me," he said, grinning. "Bit of those metals you gave me. I'll admit to skimming off the top . . ."

I looked over the pieces, and it was clear how they were meant to be worn. Copper, then iron, alloys, then silver and gold. Chien had told a story here, the story of the metals I'd brought, in small amounts, but enough to show the movement of society. There were even a few gemstones mixed in, not mana gems, but standard ones that glittered and shone in the light of the workshop. We both knew better than to wear a mana gem made from any mana but our own.

"Thank you Chien, it's magnificent."

"Look, boss, it's not for nothing. You need to make an impression now. You're an elder, and one who was more powerful than most of those old coots before you even got that white hair. They need to know that they'll respect you or you'll make them, because if they don't, you're going to have problems and we both know it. It's not just you either. They'll come after me, after Isha, after Adia, if they think they can get away with it. Now is the time to make sure they know they can't, and if they try, they'll suffer."

"I've built a fortress and manned it with some of the best people in the city. What else can I do?" I asked with a shake of my head.

"Scare the shit out of them, boss."

"Hmm, then it might be time to do something I've been thinking of for a while. I'll need a few days to get it all in order; then we'll make the official announcement. Think you can get me a few people, so that when I parade my way to the next meeting I've got a proper entourage?" I asked.

"Consider it done, boss. You mind if I join?"

"I'd be offended if you didn't, Chien. After all, you're my right hand."

“I’ll get to it then, and leave you to . . . whatever you’re planning.”

“Don’t want to help?” I asked.

“And ruin the surprise? Never.”

I laughed as he left and turned back to the tools. I’d need some of them, but then again, for this construction, I’d have to do most of it by hand.

CHAPTER 3

PARADE

The morning of my announcement, my family helped me dress. Most of it was the girls doing my hair and making sure all the jewelry was on right, but they fussed a lot, trying to make sure that everything fit perfectly. After all, there were few times when one made an announcement as big as this.

"Stay still," Isha griped as she put my hair in a braid that would best show off the one white strand.

"Yeah, stay still daddy," her little twin echoed.

"All right, all right. No need to gang up on me." They both laughed at my surrender, but kept their hands moving.

Long hair had been an on-again, off-again fashion among men over my life, and I'd had times when it had been both long and short. Now, however, I was letting it grow in anticipation of this particular event. There had been a chance that I would have gained my first white hair for the past few years, and long would show it off best.

In theory, one could keep their hair cropped short to hide their status as an elder for a while if they really felt like it. I'd heard a few stories of people doing just that, or even resorting to dyes to hide the white strands. There were many reasons for such an action—to avoid conflict with other local elders, to keep their power concealed to an extent, or even just not wanting the attention, but I'd never met anyone who had actually done it.

As I let them fiddle with the outfit, I thought back on all the people I'd known. My mother had been so close to this advancement, her and dad both, and had they made it just a few more years . . . well, perhaps they wouldn't have been there when Cino came to destroy the village. Would that have saved them? Had she gone off on her own and made her own place, would she still be here? Perhaps, perhaps not. It's possible that he'd have gone wherever they did and killed them, but who could say? It wasn't like I'd personally known the man.

What about the other elders I'd met over the years? How had they felt when they did what I was doing now? Did they meditate on it? Consider the ramifications? I wondered if they worried for what was to come as I was, or if they'd simply been thrilled to have achieved something few of us did.

And it was a sad fact that a minority of elves made it to elder status. We might not age, and might have advantages that humans of Earth hadn't, but we had problems too. Medical technology was basically nonexistent outside of magic, so if you didn't have a healer, you didn't have anything. Violence was also shockingly common, not so much amongst ourselves, but with the beasts of the wild.

Everywhere in this world were monsters, and while you were unlikely to run into one on any given day, with so many spent roving the wilds, it happened. The first I'd dealt with had been that bear, but there had been many times I could easily have died.

It wasn't surprising, then, that the well off, and those who already had magic, were the ones who tended to become elders. Though, by the time someone's first white hair appeared, everyone would have developed at least a weak form of magic to the level of being a proper mage. It was the strongest who were likely to live the hundred or so years it took to achieve the advancement in age. Sadly, the weak also tended to die not long after; having the 'authority' without the power to back it up was a recipe for disaster.

"All done," my wife finally told me, stirring me from my thoughts.

"Let's go."

I led the way, pulling open the doors and moving out of our chambers into the greater facility. As I descended into the main hall, there were gasps of surprise and wide eyes. Some of my people had known what was going on—either leaked by someone who already knew or they'd just seen me—but that was fine. It wasn't a secret. No, the surprise came from what I'd affixed to my belt.

People needed symbols, a truth that held even across worlds. Symbols united, divided, inspired. They could be the beginnings of bravery or the sign that defeat was imminent. Therefore, I'd decided that I needed a symbol, too, and only one thing stood out to me.

From my side swung a hammer. Not a warhammer, not something for battle, but something for building—a smith's hammer, a tool for advancement. It was constructed of a mixture of metals and crystals, some magical, some not, and pulsed with inner power and light. This wasn't the prototype I'd made for Atal, nor was it something I'd be using if I could avoid it, but instead a symbol, and a warning to my enemies of what would come for them should they cross me.

Chien smiled wickedly as the arranged group of aides and workers looked on.

"Ready to go, boss?" he asked.

"Yes, let us," I answered with a far firmer voice than I felt, but I needed to look strong today.

He took his spot at my right hand, with Isha to my left, just behind my shoulder, and we headed outward. Doors swung open, and the fresh air and sounds of city life rushed in. A few dozen of my people were following, chosen to come along. Others were staying behind, managing the facility and keeping an eye on my child, who would watch as we left but wasn't coming along for this.

Little Adia cheered and called from an upstairs window as I made my way across the small courtyard to the gates. This place was secure, with arrow-slits and spots for spellcasters looking down upon it. I gave her a brief smile and wave as the gates swung wide.

As my foot cleared the gate and people began looking up to see what was happening, a wave of silence spread up the road. People froze in their tracks or quickly made their way out of the street, for I was known, and they hadn't been expecting this. They all knew the results of crossing me during this procession, though, for I was going to make a statement, and weakness before such a thing would be unthinkable.

For that I was grateful, because I'd hate to have to break someone just to prove a point. I'd still do it; it was required, but I would feel bad about it later. Even if I didn't kill them, my people might, either due to some misunderstanding, or because trying to waylay such a procession would imply insult.

None did, though. The street cleared, with only a few people here and there running off. Clearly they were going to tell their bosses what was going on. That wasn't an issue. I wanted people to know, wanted them to expect what was coming.

And so I walked, the many feet crunching upon the road and the hushed whispers that a new elder was making their way forward the only sounds reaching me.

CHAPTER 4

MEETING

As I ascended the final steps to our council hall, several of my fellows stood forward to meet me. Most notable of these was Shorin, an old friend, and while not always an ally on the council, someone who at least always heard what I had to say. I smiled to him as my entourage broke off.

"Good luck, boss," Chien said as he stayed behind with the rest.

A majority of these fellows here were elders themselves, though there were a few who, like me, until recently, were not quite there yet. They were merchants, craftsmen, and experts in various fields that brought things of value to the city itself. They looked at me with wide eyes—the cloth, the jewelry, the style was what had their eyes.

The elders, though, looked elsewhere. Some looked at my hip in outright panic, the hammer hanging there something all of them knew about. Each and every one of them had either seen the battle between Atal and Cino personally, or had been present for the results, results that had lingered for some time afterward. My new hammer wasn't the same as the old one, but it was close enough that they knew what kind of things it could do if I willed it.

"Congratulations, Elder Justin," Shorin said, moving beside me as I approached, joining me instantly as a sign of his full support.

"Thank you, old friend. You don't seem overly surprised," I noted.

"I knew it was coming; sooner than I expected, but . . ." I saw him wave a quick spell around us. "Privacy."

"Something you need it for?" I asked.

"Are you planning on trying to take control of the council today? It might work, but there will be pushback, and I'd like to know before the fighting starts."

"No, I wasn't. I'm just making a point that I will be respected," I answered.

"Well, that's a load off," he said, visibly relieved. "I'd heard rumors about your ascent, but not the weapon. I can't believe you reforged it. As for respect, you'll get it with that thing hanging around."

"Too much?"

"A bit, perhaps," Shorin said with a shrug, "but it'll get attention, and stop people from complaining, so long as you don't level the hall."

I watched as one of the more militaristic elders looked on at us, eyes following our lips, no doubt trying to figure out what I was planning. As someone who hadn't had this rank before, I'd had to fight for some of my changes and was always held back by the fact that I didn't have the age. Which was nonsense. The people here knew how good my work was, and they really were just being contrarian; but coming in with a threat might well change their tune.

"You can drop the spell," I told him, and as he did, I continued. "I've no plans to; it wouldn't do anyone any good." I let the eavesdroppers make of that what they would.

The meeting hall stood where Atal's former palace had been. That building had been reworked, and though parts of it remained, it wasn't truly the same place. The palace had been for one man and his many servants, but this was for all of us. Bedrooms had been remade into offices, storage added, desks and chairs put in for people to work from and record. Other parts had been demolished, or added to. Our proper meeting hall was a rebuilt version of Atal's old throne room, now circular with tiers of seating.

In total there were about thirty of us, with a few who came and went, as needs or their desire to stay in the city waxed and waned. The younger ones were the most likely to come and go, and with my ascent, there would be five left. Nor was there a leader, as such, but rather a speaker, whose job it was to give each a turn to speak when needed.

Sadly, the speaker didn't like me. Her name was Edana, and she was among the older of the elders here, and I got to see her face go through almost every available emotion as she laid eyes upon me. First was surprise, then shock, disdain, irritation, and as her eyes made it to my waist, fear.

"Greetings, Elder Justin," she said as I took my spot. That was the minimal acknowledgment she could and would give, as the council hadn't made any declarations as of yet on the change.

Others murmured here and there, mostly the same greeting.

"Thank you, my friends," I said to them. "I hope this change is for the benefit of us all."

"Very well," our speaker said. "Onto our business then. We've received further reports of monsters from the western side of our lands. These reports are increasing in regularity and severity, as they have been for some time."

That had been going on for years. Slowly at first, but more and more as time went on, we were seeing monsters come in from the west. The earliest had been tiny, almost unnoted except in a few far-flung villages. It'd taken decades for anyone to realize anything was going on at all, much less that these rates were increasing.

"Anything new to report?" asked one of the elder members. "We've heard this before, but as far as I know, all attempts at contacting the remnants in the central region of the world have failed."

Cino's people, the few that were still left, still bore a grudge. We'd killed their leader and shattered them before driving them out, and the few who anyone had been able to find had either fled or outright refused to talk to us.

"There is," Edana said with a scowl. "We have a traveler here to speak on it."

A man was led in, young if I could judge, and rough looking. He wore ragged furs from beasts I didn't recognize and had clearly been in a number of fights, if his scars were anything to go by. His eyes scanned us almost in panic, darting about like he didn't know what to say or to whom.

"Esteemed elders," he said, bowing.

"Council members," Edana corrected him.

“Yes, apologies. Esteemed council members, I bring news. For years, my people have wandered the plains, trying to resettle, to rebuild after the loss of our old leader.”

He was one of Cino’s then? Well, probably not directly. As young as he was, I wouldn’t be surprised if he’d been born well after the ancient had fallen.

“It’s the far coastline; something there has been disturbing the beasts. Where the smoking mountains are, they expand almost by the day, the monsters who dwell in them pressing outward, sending others fleeing. They’re burning the plains, leaving nothing but ash and death. I came as a last attempt, to beg for aid.”

“Perhaps we should send an envoy to see what is going on. Justin, I believe you’ve traveled through that region before, no?” Edana asked.

“I have, but I am indisposed currently,” I informed her and all others.

“It wouldn’t be too long, though. The mission would be—”

“No.” I infused my voice with a slight bit of magic to enhance it. In the past I might have had to explain why, or deal with objections or complaints, but now I would entertain none of it. The one word alone, louder than it should have been, silenced the hall.

CHAPTER 5

BETS AGAINST THE FUTURE

After my display, the other elders left me to my devices, which was good. Perhaps they were voicing their irritation behind closed doors, but none were bringing it to me, and that was excellent because I wasn't in the mood to deal with them. I had other far more important things to do.

"Would you like more tea?" asked my daughter, offering forward the tiny kettle she had. It actually contained tea, not just pretend. It was, however, a cold blend, not a piping hot one.

"Certainly." I accepted, filling my cup as I looked around at all the small chairs near me, filled with her favorite toys.

Isha had thought I was being silly giving her all these as she grew up, but it was too adorable to do otherwise. Adia and I had a daily tea party, where she took her time to tell me all about her day and what had been going on.

Most of what she told me was what she and her friends had been doing, or complaints about her lessons from one of her teachers, and I listened to all of it. We lived a long time, and these were years I was never getting back, so I didn't want to miss a single second, not a moment that I could file in my timeless memories to replay when she was older. I didn't want her to miss anything, either, for though her daddy might have been a very busy man, he always had time for her, and I needed her to know that. After all, she and Isha were the two most important people in my life. Wouldn't it do for them to know it?

"I don't want to do more math," she complained. This one I got often.

"I know, but it is useful, and it doesn't take long."

"How? Why do I need to know it?" What she was on now was really just basic addition and subtraction, but she still hated the lessons.

"You know how your mother keeps track of things," I said. "Don't you want to know what she's doing?" Isha was in charge of the finances for the compound, managing it like a hawk.

"I've seen the things she does, and this doesn't look like that," she pouted, motioning to the small numbers written on the blackboard I'd provided for her teachers.

"One thing builds upon another, like making a house of blocks. You need to start with the base first, and then you can get to bigger and better things."

"You don't have to do lessons," she pointed out.

I laughed at that. "Not like yours, but I am always learning. One day you'll be like that, too, learning, but without a teacher to lead you."

"Want to do that now."

"Don't wish for that Adia."

"Why not?"

"Because when you're big like that things won't be the same, and I'll miss these days."

"Don't understand."

"One day you will." I leaned forward and kissed the top of her head.

"Can we play more tomorrow? You've been in your room too much." That was a valid complaint. I had been working more than usual, and a break would be nice.

"I think I can do that," I told her. "Think about what you want to play."

She smiled and took a sip of her tea before going on about her friends. She didn't have too many of those. Most were children of people who worked for me, or the kids of others whom Isha and I were friends with.

It was a bit sad, but there were relatively few children in the entire city. That was an issue for our whole species, and one I didn't know what to do about. It was obvious we needed some kind of proper schooling, as many of them knew very little, and with our memories, it would be breakneck fast to teach them quite a lot.

Schools and education was something I'd put forward to the council before, and it had been vetoed, but that didn't mean I'd given up. I'd taught a few people some basics, and put them to tutoring the children of my employees, and later my own daughter. Learning these things would bring them forward into real professions sooner. If we could build the base, we could build so high.

Once Adia had finished her explanations, I excused myself back to my workrooms. There was a time for everything, and with the report we'd gotten, I had a few things I wanted to work on.

"You sure this will work, boss?" Chien asked as I came in, overlooking some of my plans.

"You've seen the models, no?" I asked, pointing to the smaller versions hovering over a patch of the floor, little strings keeping them in place.

"I believe you are the one who told me that when things get bigger, they change sometimes."

"A fair point, and I'm not completely sure, but I think it will do. When should we have the materials for it?" I asked.

"Um . . . I don't know. The cloth is likely to be the real problem, even if we got all of it for the whole city we'd still be short. I'm also not sure that what we have will work for something so large, even that weird carbon cloth stuff you've made."

"Well, see what we can do. I'll start work on my version, but we will need a lot. I want this ready in case something goes wrong."

"All right, boss. I'll get on it."

The plans for what could only be described as a blimp sprawled across my desk. If I was being honest, I was guessing on much of this, working the best I could with what I knew, and it was sure to be a bit rough around the edges. However, I wanted something, for if we were getting worse and worse monsters coming from the west, I might need to act, and acting from above and at a high speed would be far better than any ground-based assault I could think of.

Planes had been an option, too, but I knew next to nothing about how to design one of those. Sure, I knew the wing shape, but I also knew they were far more technical, and we didn't have that backing yet. We had no engines, no aluminum for a good body, no proper wing materials, and if it failed, it would fall like a stone. With a blimp I was just floating on gasses, gasses that could potentially fail, but I'd give myself much better odds if they did. I also didn't need to explain how I knew a plane would work—something someone would decidedly ask me.

There was another addition I wasn't sure how to put on a plane either, sitting in one corner of my shop. The cannon was massive, built around the idea of contained, magically generated explosions. It, too, was getting tested soon, for if there was something big coming, we'd want something nasty to counter it.

CHAPTER 6

PREPARING

For the first time in a long time, I was getting to do some proper forging myself. I loved it, the heat, the way the metal bent, the cherry red shade it could turn under the flame. It wasn't my favorite thing in the world, but as a side hobby, it was magnificent. It was also very physical, something working with computers, magical or otherwise, really wasn't.

Most of what I was doing now was being formed magically, large parts of the frame for my first airship being pulled in and set before me. Some of the smaller parts, however, I needed to do by hand. Perhaps one day we'd have a machine for it, but for now a jig and anvil would do.

As I finished each, I put them to the side with the others in my workshop. There would be hundreds of them, so this wasn't a project I'd be finishing anytime soon, but that didn't mean I couldn't put the work in. In fact, the faster I got it done, the sooner it would be ready. All bonuses, so far as I could tell.

It had been several weeks since I'd started this project in earnest, and as I found myself hammering away in my lab, a bell rang. I looked up and saw that it was one from upstairs, a small spot on the wall indicating where someone had come to call for me. That was odd, as normally the only people who'd interrupt my work for nonemergency reasons were my family or Chien, yet this one came from the main entryway. The tone they'd used didn't indicate emergency, just a need for my attention.

With no further alerts, I took my time to set things so they wouldn't cause problems if I needed to walk away for the day, putting metal where it could safely cool and turning off forges before I walked to my door.

As I made my way to the entry, I saw a very flustered assistant looking on at a clearly unhappy elf, and one I recognized.

"Jina?" I asked. "It's quite a surprise to see you here."

The woman in question was the granddaughter of the former ruler of Atal, and quite possibly one of the oldest of the elders in this region. She'd taught me many of the basics surrounding magical items, at the behest of her forefather, and while I wouldn't say we were friends, we at least knew each other.

"Made me wait long enough," she groused. Clearly, the many years since I'd seen her hadn't improved her generally grumpy demeanor.

"Is there something you needed immediately?" I asked. "I thought you were staying at the old village."

"I was, am, but things have gotten to a point where I felt the need to come and speak with you."

"The other elders bothering you that much? I'm not going out to investigate whatever is going on." She frowned at my words, but I still wasn't changing my stance. I'd promised my wife that I'd abstain from any more "adventures" until our child was grown, and I planned to keep that promise.

"They didn't need to, not with how things have been."

That was a concerning statement. The last time I'd seen Jina, she'd taken up vigil watching a certain cave near where I'd grown up, one which contained a danger not even I felt comfortable dealing with. Deep down beneath the ground was what looked like an impact from a meteor and a font of eggs in mana-charged water that had been a major point of power in the last war. Our enemy had used it to create suicide soldiers from our children, youths charged up with power their bodies couldn't safely contain, and whom he threw at us in droves.

"Is the cave . . ."

"Safe for now, but the number of beasts in the woods isn't to be misunderstood. I came to the city to seek some aid, only to be told that you'd flatly refused to do anything at all on the subject."

Good grief, they'd been unable to run and tell my mommy that I didn't want to do their chore, so they'd found the next best thing. That thought pinged once more about her loss, fouling my mood further, and convincing me that at some point I would need to reassert that I wasn't to be messed with.

"I haven't refused to do *anything*; I've refused to do the thing they want," I replied after a few moments.

"Why?" she asked, seeming almost genuinely interested.

"Firstly, I do not need to explain myself to you. Secondly, because I made a promise. If they're that bothered they could've come to me themselves, but it appears that our little council is full of cowards and fools."

"You're on it," she pointed out.

"True, but only because I want to be left alone. Have you not heard that a committee is the only warm-blooded creature with more than two legs and no brain?" Of course she hadn't, because that was from Earth, but it held true here, too.

"No," she said with a snorting laugh, "but I'll admit, I like that one. Still, I would like you to put forth some aid. We both know that you're capable." She motioned to my home/fortress as she spoke.

"Let's continue this elsewhere," I said, turning and leading her along to one of my offices. I really didn't want to extend this argument in my atrium any more than I needed to.

"Fine."

She followed, looking around at my home, and it struck me. She still looked like we had years ago, and I'd barely noticed. She wore furs, cleaned and held together with ties and simple buttons; her hair, half white, was beaded; and her shoes were little more than wraps. Yet, here I was, walking in a simple robe of cloth, through a home that could have easily been medieval in nature. All along the floors were patterned tiles in a variety of colors, with archways of stone or cement. There were even rugs on the floors in some places, with elves walking around in basic uniforms we'd provided. It was so anachronistic that I almost laughed.

"Your home is almost like grandfather's," she noted as we walked along. "No, it's different; he never had many of these things. Yet it speaks the same language, the same trappings of power. Tell me, do you wish to become like he was?"

"To rule? I'm happy to let others take care of all that," I replied. "I mostly want to be let be. I suppose one day I might, but let's not rush that."

When we finally got to the office, I showed her to a seat, and it struck me again. She was here, a cave woman in all but name, joining me in my office for discussions on how to deal with a horde of monsters. Life really was strange sometimes, and I wondered if one day we'd be having times like these, except in giant steel and glass towers. That really would be something.

"Let's speak frankly. I'm not going to do what the council wants," I told her.

"Yet?"

"Yet, that doesn't mean I'm doing nothing. It's been some time, but I'm preparing for war again."

Jina flinched, breathing in. I saw her eyes lose focus and knew she was reliving memories, memories of the last time I'd gone to war.

"Do you need help?" she inquired after a time.

"I wouldn't mind it this time, and you're actually in a perfect place to do so."

I began to form a plan, one that might serve both our interests, and those of my fellow elders, though I doubted they'd like it.

CHAPTER 7

CATCHING UP

There were different levels of elders, and while it was a group I'd just joined, Jina was an old, old hand to it. That was partly why I needed her.

"So you want me to reinforce our entire border?" she asked as we moved through the conversation. "I don't hate the idea, but I believe you're overestimating my abilities."

"That's because I don't want you to do it alone. If we've got waves of monsters coming in, we need to stop them, and the council needs to be convinced to send people to do just that, rather than just someone to figure out what is going on. They won't listen to me, but I doubt they'll ignore you if you push for it. They're not stupid enough to risk you coming in and taking over the whole city."

"Doing that might not be the worst thing you've ever proposed," she mumbled.

"No, it would. You'd hate it, and we both know it. In a week, you'd be killing people just to shut them up."

"And you wouldn't?" she asked, and I didn't feel the need to comment.

"We also probably don't need to worry about the whole border, mostly just the western edge, and even then, the mountains will help a lot. Those damn things have been a barrier to our people for as long as anyone can remember, and I don't doubt that the beasts everyone's complaining about are coming through the few passes that actually make it through them. Close those gaps, and we should see the numbers plummet."

"And what exactly will you be doing to help? I've heard you say you were readying to, but no evidence of it."

"You doubt that I'm preparing things?" I asked.

"No, but others might, and telling them what you're doing will settle them, particularly if they understand it."

"They wouldn't, though," I pointed out.

"People are more clever than you give them credit for. Even if you only show me what you're up to, it'll be enough for me to tell them you're doing something."

"I'm making a platform for weapons, one we can fight and scout safely from."

"That's hardly difficult to understand."

"How it works isn't, and the fact is that it will take me several seasons to finish it, at least. Even then, it's only a proof, like the first weapons I made for your grandfather, enough to show that it can be done."

"So it could fail?"

"Yes, it could. I'm fairly sure that it won't, but this is all new to me, and so it could."

"Still, I'd like to see it."

I shrugged. That was fine, as there was nothing in that particular workshop she could make mischief with right now. So, we took a quick walk and soon found ourselves in my workspace, her eyes growing wide at the piles and piles of metal pieces I'd been making for some time now.

"That is so much metal," Jina whispered as she took it all in. "All the tools, all the weapons that it could make."

"It's quite a bit, but just because I'm using it for this project doesn't mean weapons and tools aren't getting made. Even in the other shops here they're doing that kind of thing now, and you forget, I'm no longer the only one who can work with metal like this. Others are making things, too, heaps and heaps of them."

It was easy to see her surprise, and to understand it. While I might be able to get literal tons of steel and bronze now, that wasn't the case everywhere. Even most of the other metalworkers in the city couldn't get the sheer amounts that I used casually, and they were sought after. Outside of Atal, metal and those who could do anything with it were still exceedingly rare. In the whole of the western half of our lands there was probably less steel—maybe even metal in general—than was in this room alone.

The knowledge was spreading—that wasn't to be misunderstood—and the items were, too, but that didn't mean they were doing it fast. Without me around to guide and challenge them, a lot of the smiths had become complacent, and once I'd returned from my previous journey, I had things I was doing rather than teaching. So the average metalworker was taking their sweet time, and not one of them could match me for how much of the stuff I was gathering at once.

"If we'd had this for the war?" she asked.

"This took time to build, Jina, and reflecting on what could have been won't help. At any rate, while these tools are great, they wouldn't have matched the magic."

She nodded. "Thank you. So, what is all of this?"

"A frame," I explained. Frames were something people had used even before I arrived in this world, either for houses or for other tools.

"It's going to be . . . very large."

It was going to be a small, but still a functionally sized blimp. "Yes."

"Very well, I'll tell your council you've convinced me that you're doing what you need to. Please, though, don't go too far."

"I try not to."

She laughed at that, really laughed.

"You fail."

"Maybe, but I do try. Mind if I ask about something else now?"

"What?"

"How's the village? Did those women end up resettling?"

"They did, though, if you wanted to know that, you could have visited. They're doing well; most of the original group is no more, but that doesn't surprise me. They were never right after what happened to them, and while some of them tried to heal, the young always seem to die. It's so much worse when they're injured like that, too." She looked sad as she spoke.

"You didn't help them?" I asked.

“I did some, but at a certain point you have to let little birds fly. You’ll understand in another century or two, I think. If you coddle them too much, they’re stunted and can never really soar like they should.”

“You said most were gone, so some lived, I suppose.”

“Indeed they did. One of the ones who was a child when you came through has grown into a leader now. Rather than collapse into her own mind or lash out, she used her pain to build.”

“That’s good to hear. Perhaps one day we’ll meet.”

CHAPTER 8

✧

BEASTS OF BLOOD

Construction of my first flying machine was proceeding apace, and by that I mean slowly. There was so much that went into any sizable build that it took time and patience. Oddly, some of the other elders in the city had too little of the latter, which one would think wouldn't be the case for people who were literally ageless.

I received questions pretty much daily on what I was doing and how it would work, and when it would be done. Eventually, I just stopped even bothering to pretend to answer them. Instead, I told the messengers to shove off; or if the elder in question had taken the time to learn to write, I burned their letters.

Writing, at least, had caught on to some degree. Many people still thought it was a very niche skill, but with how we could remember things, learning to read took literal minutes, and writing, not much longer. Penmanship had failed to catch on yet, though, so most writing looked like it had come from a first-grade classroom. However, I knew my people, and we liked to do things well, so I had no doubt that soon things would get far better.

"Did you secure the second site?" I asked Chien as he entered my workshop.

"Sure did, boss," he told me. "Think we'll need all that room, though?"

"Yes, this thing is gonna be big. The cloth as well?"

"I've got it. You know I'm surprised that you're letting me take care of that on my own."

"You've earned my trust, Chien. If you say you've got it, I assume you've got it."

"Aww, I'm touched."

"Honestly, you could probably take the project from here if you wanted to. Would you like to?" I asked.

"No, but why do you ask?" He saw my eyes flick toward the back part of my workshop, the sealed door nobody but I was allowed in and sighed. "Seriously, boss? That thing is doomed isn't it? I know you want it to work, but I'm just not seeing it."

"If I could just get it to hold and release the mana, it would be there. I can even use it to a limited form now, but without the ability to store anything . . ."

The object in question was one of my attempts at making a magical computer. It was very, very proto, but that wasn't the point. If I could just get it to function, I could explode our society into the future. Nobody here realized how important the ability to parse that much data that fast would be. In my old world it had been able to do wonders, and here, with magic, we could bypass so, so many of the steps in putting it to use.

"Maybe your approach is wrong? Not that I'd know where to go with it, but we don't have time anyway, if you want this project done."

"What are you talking about?" I asked. "I've got plenty of time until you get these taken to the other site."

I turned to indicate the frame pieces. They were as near to complete as they could be without putting them together, stacked one on top of the other, measured, bent, and ready. So long as they weren't broken in transit or lost, we could start building the outer shell right away. There would still be the needed envelope and the carriage for the people to ride in, but the balloon part was really getting close to ready.

"Oh, really? Even after the scout has returned?"

"What? When was this? Has it sincerely been that long?" Thinking back, it had been a few months, enough for dedicated runners to make it to Rolan and back, but not really see too much.

"Why do you think I came down here? I appreciate your work and all, but you hardly need my input for this."

"Bah," I grumbled as I gathered up my things to head to the old palace. If the scout they'd sent was back already, then I needed to hear what he had to say.

The room stretched out around us, the rows of leaders all looking inward, all looking to the light, wiry elf that had been sent away and returned with a haunted look. I'd gotten here as soon as I'd heard of his return, but I still had to wait for hours for the full presentation, giving others time to interrogate him and work their own plans into place.

"So," the head of our gathering said, "tell us what you've seen."

Three Weeks Earlier

"Careful, Sochu. I can almost feel it from here," my companion, Lilien, said, peeking up and around the rocks.

"Don't worry, I just need to get much further, just get a view."

Over the last couple of weeks we'd found less and less. It was clear that the people of the plains were fleeing as fast as they could eastward, abandoning villages and setting up shelters close to the base of the mountains, and it became clear why. Whole villages were burned to ash, paths in the beaten dirt the only sign they'd ever existed. Other sections of the plains were still aflame from the fleeing monsters, wildfires burning out of control across land that shouldn't have supported such blazes, only kept going by the herds of beasts stalking within the firestorms.

Many of these creatures were coming from the flaming mountains, bare stretches of blasted rock and rivers of melted stone, and they needed the flames to live. They thrived in the heat, and I suspected would die like a flower in winter if it grew too cold. However, their needs didn't make them any less dangerous.

The only question was what was driving them this way, and it was a question we needed to answer and chase west to find the cause. So we did, running through scorched fields, avoiding what we could. There were few streams or rivers among the endless grasses, or what had been grasses—a challenge for stopping the spread of the fire and an issue for our resupply of water.

My legs pumped up the scrabble of the mountainside. There were few places along the western mountains where we could get over, and fewer that I would want to. This ridge, however, was high enough that nothing on the far side was likely to see me, and if it did, it would be less likely to be able to get to me here. After all, there had been few beasts crossing in this particular section, evidenced by the small growths of new grass at the mountain's base.

As I got to the top, I found a sheer cliff; not tall—perhaps four times my own height—and I began to climb, fingers as strong as stone digging in and pulling me up. I could hang by one alone if I needed to, my speed and strength almost equal to that of an elder.

The crest had a small, flat top, enough for me to look down and see over the barriers and onto the other side. What I found chilled my bones. We'd seen burning lands on this side, places consumed by flames, but the far side of these mountains was different. Nothing grew that I could see—bare rock stretched nearly to the horizon. Tall, almost glassy stones rose, and along the landscape an orange ribbon flowed like a snake, slithering through the land. Smoke rose here and there, too, spraying from rends and cracks in the ground.

None of that compared to the corpses though. Everywhere I looked were strewn the charred remains of massive, hulking beasts. Things that looked like turtles or odd lizards were broken and burned—not even eaten, just ripped apart—with a few bearing claw or bite marks. It was like they'd all been slaughtered, and soon I found the killers.

Among the carnage were two enormous creatures, lizards of some kind, currently engaged in ripping apart a beast that had glowing rocks along its back. They harried it, striking and slashing with claws. For its part, the other monster seemed to desire only to flee to the river of lava, striking only enough to push them back for a moment so it could run.

Gauging size was impossible from this height. With no frame of reference for any of the creatures, I couldn't possibly give an accurate account, but they were all massive; that much, at least, I could see. Their strikes rended the stones upon the ground, leaving gouges and scrapes where it had been smooth.

As I looked on, the two lizards grabbed and pulled, with coordination that spoke to some form telepathic communication. They managed to flip their enemy before ripping apart its belly. But why they were doing this, I couldn't guess because they spent mere moments engaged in that pastime before jumping back. As the blood dried upon their muzzles, they looked around, searching, hunting, but why?

I watched them for a couple of hours. Together they searched, pulling apart the ground and checking wherever they could, looking for anything else, but finding no other living creature. Then, one of them changed, waiting until his companion stuck his snout into a rock formation, and then charging at the other monster's back.

Their fight was bloody, brutal, and brief. In seconds it seemed one had ripped the throat from the other, leaving his previous ally to die upon the stone as he threw back his head and screeched to the sky. Then came other screams, a terrible keening just like the one I had heard. The monster turned its head, going toward what seemed to be the nearest.

As I returned to my companion, he looked at me with fear in his eyes. "You look bad."

"We need to go now." Without further preamble, I turned east. Those things hadn't yet made it across the barrier of the high cliffs, and when they did, I had no doubt they would hunt anything and everything they could. That was why the beasts were fleeing toward us. They were all running for their lives.

CHAPTER 9

REACTIONS

As the scout finished his account, we all stood stunned. Beasts that seemed devoted to nothing but killing, and ones that were the size he described, were almost unheard of. Sadly, *almost* was an operative word, as there were monsters like that in this world. Large monsters came and went, mostly sticking to defined, remote territories until, and unless, they were in some change of their life.

The killing was the most concerning part. To many, it might have seemed as if it was just random, but to those of us who'd heard the stories, those of us old enough to know, it was clear. These creatures weren't just slaughtering to slaughter; they were slaughtering because they needed the territory. Mixed with the fact that they'd just shown up, this told us they would be growing and soon.

It was like a pond with thousands and thousands of spawn laid in it. Be they frog spawn or fish spawn, or even insects, they would devour all those around them as they grew, and they would also devour each other, until only the largest and strongest survived. In a pool of thousands of frog spawn, there might be only a few to make it to adulthood, but those adults would be something else when compared to their infant forms.

What would these things be when they were done? What would they become? I didn't know. Perhaps they were the ancestors of the beasts, whose bones lay in the cave below my first home, but that didn't make sense. No, those creatures had wings, whereas these had none; and while I couldn't rule out the possibility of them going through some transformation, it just didn't seem likely to me.

"So what do we do?" asked Shorin.

"We must send someone to deal with this before it gets out of hand. I've only heard stories, but those stories suggest these creatures will get larger and larger until they're destroyed." It was the speaker Edana who'd suggested that, though not who should go.

"No," I interrupted before one of them tried to suggest me. "We should send messengers to the nearby ancients. They have lived longer than us, and may well know what these creatures are. They may also be planning to deal with them themselves."

"What brings you to that conclusion?" Edana asked, turning to me.

"They're closer to Matriarch Neera's lands, and Rolan seems to me the responsible type. If they don't already know of the issue, they will want to, and if they do, they're likely making their own preparations."

"You suggest we hide behind one of them?" accused another of my fellows, one of the older elders who didn't much like me.

"If you think you have the power of an ancient, feel free to go oppose one of them. Otherwise, be silent," I told him. We were of the same station now, so there was no need for me to even bother being polite to someone stupid.

And it was stupid; there were limits to what we could do. Sure, I might be able to hack together something that could fight even these things; and I was, in fact, working on doing just that, but it didn't change that all such things I put together would be a trick, not a thousands-of-years-old warrior. Tricks worked, but in cases like this, it would still be best to consult a professional.

"Who shall we send then?" Edana said, eyes slipping toward me.

"You've a messenger here; send him. I'll do what I can to prepare, should we need to fight these creatures ourselves. None of them seem likely to be as strong as an ancient ready to go to war, but perhaps we can manage something."

I didn't even bother acknowledging what she clearly wanted, what they all did. They were still afraid, and for good reason; if I were ready, I could probably take all of them. They were also cowards and sincerely getting on my nerves. After all, if I'd wanted to take the city, I'd have made my move long ago.

I wanted to scoff. If I had known what a right pain in the ass they would be, I might have considered taking over Atal. I might still have to if I wanted to be left alone, but for now that seemed unnecessary, so I avoided thinking too much about it. Still, the idea of Isha and I in the palace that she certainly deserved did poke its head into my thoughts; and before I knew it, I was beginning to design the place—rooms, halls, what materials to use.

"Justin, did you have an answer?" The mention of my name stirred me from my daydreaming, and I quickly played back the conversation in my mind. Being an elf certainly had its advantages.

"Weeks, maybe months before my current project is complete. It all depends on getting the right cloth in the correct amounts," I informed the council.

"My niece is in a village making that stuff. Should I call her and ask to change over to what you need?" a member asked, helpfully.

The rest of the meeting was much like that, questions of supply and who needed to do what. Mostly, I sat back, answering a few questions now and again. Other people needed to prepare, too, and I was glad to see they were doing so. The leaders of the city guard were working on adding to the walls and increasing the number of siege weapons they had. The casters were talking about training and tattooing those who could be of use. Someone even brought up the idea of boats to flee with—not a terrible idea.

Sadly, my own experiments in boating had been limited in use, at best. There was a lot that went into it, and frankly, I didn't understand it well enough to be of use. Could I have figured something seaworthy out? Maybe, but I didn't want to; it wasn't interesting to me.

By the time I got home, I was tired and headed straight for my workshop. There were always things to do. As the door began to close behind me, I heard someone.

"Absolutely not, you need to rest."

Turning, I saw my wife headed my way, and she was alone, so she could only be speaking to me.

"If I must, then come join me," I said, motioning her inside.

Isha seldom joined me in my workshop, and by seldom, I mean never. With a pout she tried to pull me away, but seeing that wasn't working, she just came along. It was cute how she sometimes got like this—angry that I was too busy.

"You've improved it," she said, looking around as we entered.

"Quite a bit. It's been what, forty years since you came in here?"

"Something like that. I didn't realize you'd made it so much bigger."

"Want me to show you around?"

CHAPTER 10

ANOTHER SET OF HANDS

Isha was mostly uninterested in my fabrication facilities, such as they were. Most of the things I did, I did with purely magic, having neither the know-how nor the tools for machining things. Instead, a lot of my work was cast or forged, shaped by will and hard blows.

However, she was interested in the materials, of which I had many. I'd searched my memories for anything useful, any recipe that I might manage to remake. Most of those had been abject failures, with no ability on my part to find the right things, or just no knowledge of the details that were important to most modern things. I did have glass of many colors, though, metals and fibers that weren't available anywhere else, and paper better than anywhere in this world could produce. There was also a bit of detailed pottery of various types—experiments that I kept mostly because pots were nostalgic to me.

"What are these?" she asked, picking up an attempt at a plastic bottle and looking at it thoughtfully.

"A failure, sadly. I made them from cooking oil, but they don't work." It had a stopper rather than a twist cap and was on one of the tables where I kept my failures.

"Why not?"

"Dissolves, and I don't know why."

There were a lot of things like that, creations that I'd made but just couldn't get working. They were neat, very neat, but I was no chemical engineer and had neither the training, nor had I read the reference materials I'd need for that sort of thing. That didn't stop me from trying, of course, but more often than not, it was just a poor attempt, worse than even a child on Earth could've made with access to the internet and a grocery store.

"I'm sure you'll get it," she said, patting me on the arm lightly.

We spent a long time looking at gems; she liked them. Pretty much everyone liked shiny rocks, my wife included, and even more when they could be shaped and counted as money. It was an interesting thing, money. When I'd first come to Atal, beads had been the trading currency, with nicer ones being worth exponentially more, and it was much the same now.

The main difference now, though, was that the wood, stone, and pottery beads that had once been the staples were now something akin to nickels and dimes. Replacing them were beads of copper, or iron; these were less decorated but could be made readily into useful materials. Most were even of an almost standardized size and weight. Still, though, particularly beautiful pieces like those I could make. If I tried, they would be worth quite a bit.

Perhaps one day I could convince the council to go change over to an actual currency. Heck, we could even use beads if they wanted to—just make them ourselves at a given size and let people go from there. You know, actually, if I started doing that myself, making them and then using them for everyone—

"What's over there?" Isha pointed, stirring me from my thoughts of changing policy by forcing it.

"Hmm?" I followed her finger to the door on the side, the one I kept locked. "Oh, that's my computer project."

"The thinking item?" she asked. I'd tried to explain the idea to her once, but hadn't really gotten too far before she seemed thoroughly bored.

"Sort of," I replied. "It doesn't really think, just looks like it does from the outside, kind of."

"You're bad at explanations. Can I see it?" she asked.

"If you want, but there's not much to look at."

I had to manually put mana into the door to open it, the lock clicking as I pulled it away from the wall. This room was extraordinarily simple, clean white panels, with a few lights and dials worked into several of them. There was nothing like the screens and visual interfaces that were so familiar to the people of Earth, and there didn't need to be. A few sections that displayed sets of numbers was where I was currently at, unable to get much further until I had something that worked.

The only thing of real note was the small dais in the center of the room, upon which sat a small gem, surrounded by the many lines that connected it to the rest of the apparatuses. The actual computer itself was tiny, since I didn't really need it any bigger, and would probably be invisible to the naked eye, if I'd not mounted it on a piece about the size of a postage stamp.

"You weren't joking," Isha said. "What is all this?" She looked around the very plain room, a big change from the rest of my workspace.

"If I can get it working, it'll be the start of the greatest thing I've ever made. Sadly, no matter what, I can't get it to work. I need a way to make it hold and use magic, but it won't, no matter what I do. Sure, I can get this whole place to work while I feed magic to it, like the tattoos, but it quickly fades, and doesn't have the . . . abilities I need it to."

"The only reason the tattoos hold magic at all is that they are worked into you. They're a part of the person when it's all done, inside the bits that make you up."

"What?! Where did you learn that?" I asked.

"You're not the only one with friends, Justin. I talk to people, too, and learn things." She looked a bit peeved as she spoke, frowning.

"Sorry, it's just, I've never heard that. Makes sense, though, since they have to interact with your body—"

"Anyway, what's all this do?" she asked, pointing to the various displays.

"Communicates with the computer," I explained as simply as I could. "It speaks a language of numbers, so you have to translate to something people can understand. These take those numbers and put them in a form that makes any sense to people." At least I'd upgraded from the breadboards I was using before, something that really didn't look like much more than a collection of wires.

"If it's not intelligent, how can it speak?" she asked.

"Eh . . . it isn't really speaking; that's just the explanation. It mostly uses . . . something like a card with one color on one side and another color on the other side. By putting in the right set of instructions, you get it to put the cards in the right order. The whole thing is modular, with the ability to expand to a limited degree. The one I have here would just be the first section, then it would get bigger and bigger until it could do some truly amazing things."

"You're losing the point again."

"Sorry, it's just a lot to explain without getting into the deepest parts." Trying to find context for something that had no paradigm here was hard.

"All right, can I help?" she asked.

"Do you want to?" I was taken aback by that question, since she seldom seemed all that interested in my work.

"Why would I have asked otherwise?"

CHAPTER 11

OVERSIZED ISSUES

With my wife now aiding me, I gave her a lot of documentation and got back to what I was actually supposed to be doing. I felt bad about having to put together and then dump upon her so much info, but she had asked for it. It also wasn't like I was actually expecting her to do anything more than whatever she felt like. If she took years to read those documents, that would be perfectly fine with me.

There was ultimately no reason for me to tell her no. It wasn't like I didn't trust her with anything. Even if she messed something up, which, given her personality, she seemed unlikely to do, it didn't matter. I could rebuild all that I currently had from memory with minimal effort. After all, I'd been all but stuck for years. On the off chance that she did figure something out, then all the better.

As for me, though, I needed to start moving out. Our secondary site had been determined, provided by none other than Jina.

We needed a place, and she'd taken care of it. How many heads she'd had to bash to make that happen I didn't know and didn't want to, but since it was technically outside the city walls, the council had no say at all in it.

"So what's the verdict?" I asked Chien as he returned from scouting out the new location.

"It's rough, but it'll do for what we need. Did you know that your friend can grow impossibly large trees seemingly from nothing? Because she can, like stories tall and all interwoven. The whole place is one giant plant from what I can tell."

"I'll have to tell her how helpful that was. I was just expecting an empty field."

"Well, I think the old lady wants these issues solved so she can go back to her curmudgeoning, or whatever it is she does. Having monsters come to her home, or having to deal with the gaggle of idiots who run this city—no offense—doesn't seem to be her speed."

"It's not anyone's speed. I hate dealing with the gaggle of idiots who run this city."

"Even yourself?"

"Particularly myself. I'm a massive pain who keeps coming up with new ideas that he needs to put into practice. If not for me, do you know how much free time I would have?"

He belted out a hearty laugh.

"On another note, how go the attempts at getting me my cloth?"

"Ongoing, boss. The workshops are at it, but you know how long these things take."

"Fair enough."

We headed out so I could check the site personally, and I had to admit, Jina had outdone herself. The inside was easily thirty meters tall, more than enough for this first dirigible. As far as the other dimensions, it had more than enough space on all sides. More impressive was that I hadn't told her how big it needed to be. Could she just see the pieces of the skeleton and figure it out? Could I do that? Questions I needed to figure out later.

As he'd told me, the whole thing was grown into place. The trees reminded me of the ones I'd seen to the north—massive pillars of wood. However, these were right atop each other, and held together with interwoven branches, the same ones that made the ceiling. I briefly wondered if those could be removed at some point. If they couldn't, we could still take the final product out through the front, but it would be cool if we didn't.

"Good enough?" Chien asked.

"More than enough, my friend, more than. Let's start moving everything over. We may need to add a few small workshops in the area, depending on how things go, but this should work perfectly."

"So when are we going to get the frame here, and how?" Chien asked.

"We can start in the morning, and what do you mean how? I have doors, don't I?" There were, in fact, doors for unloading things. They were a bit of a pain to open, but plenty large enough for big projects to leave my shop.

"What I meant was the length. Won't the walls get in the way?"

I thought for a moment, picturing the whole layout, and winced. He was right. I'd made plenty of large projects, but never one this long.

"You didn't think about it at all, did you?"

"Honestly, no."

"Well, what about removing one of the walls? We could make a hole all the way out to the street and just push the pieces through." It was a good suggestion, but not that good.

"Pretty sure those walls are structural," I said. "We'll need to add supports, and . . . crap."

"You know, boss, for someone so smart, sometimes you make dumb mistakes."

"Like you've never done something like this," I argued.

"There was that one time with the cart . . ."

Over the next few hours we put together a plan, like how and where to remove the long, steel pieces of frame from my home. Then, the city itself, which was less of a problem, but I didn't want to risk it. With our memories, we worked through each and every problem we could foresee, making a few models. Through our combined knowledge, we came to the conclusion that we'd only need to rip out three walls, and a door, from the house to get them out.

Then, it was my turn to laugh, because the best way to get them out was ironically through Chien's personal rooms. That certainly wasn't planned, but I was going to take the wins where I could get them.

CHAPTER 12

✧

SNACKS AND THINKING ROCKS

Adia

I crept from room to room, looking, watching. Mommy was somewhere, and if I was going to get to the kitchens and get any snacks, I'd need to keep her from seeing me. She didn't like it when I got snacks in the middle of the day.

Daddy was helping, too. With all the noise and trouble he was making, breaking whole walls while people tried to pull out . . . big long things, and take them out of the house. He was silly, always doing things like that.

I wanted to move around his mess to get what I wanted, using all the people being busy to escape, but Uncle Chien was over there, and he told me not to get near. Daddy might be silly, but Uncle Chien was always looking out for me, seeing me around corners and behind things. He watched the auras—the little lights everyone had—and used them to pick me out. If he said I wasn't allowed and he found me sneaking about, he'd definitely hand me over to Mommy.

So, I worked my way around the big mess, letting the noise cover me, slinking across the floor like a shadow. I was a shadow, still and quiet, nobody paying attention. A few of the workers here passed, smiling, but they didn't see me, their eyes going over me like I wasn't here as they snickered to each other.

"Have you seen Isha around?" one of them asked loudly in front of the box I was hiding behind.

"Oh, I'm sure she's around here somewhere. She'll probably be going to Miss Adia's room in a bit to make sure she's studying like she should," his coworker told him, also so loud that everyone would hear them.

"Okay, well let's be off then."

They left, and I poked my head out from behind the box, smiling as they'd missed me before I continued on. Hall by hall I moved, past workshops and offices. It was fun to be out and hiding like this.

Soon enough, I made it to the kitchen, pressed against the wall as I looked in. A small bowl of sweet fruit sat on a counter there, ripe and ready. Abandoning my hiding place, I ran forward, hopping first on a chair, and then close enough on the counter to reach out and wrap my fingers around one.

"Got you," came a voice, as I was snatched from behind, right as my fingers wrapped around my prize.

"No!" I called out, pulling the snack up to my face and munching down.

"Sincerely, Adia?" Mommy asked. "You're just as much a mess as your father."

"That's not true! Daddy's way more silly than I am," I declared as I continued to eat, dodging left and right as she reached for the food I was shoving in my mouth.

"Hard to argue with that, but if you were hungry, you could have just asked," she said as she gave up taking my prize and hauled me off.

"You would've said no, and you've been all busy." I could only talk between bites, but she seemed to understand.

"I would've said no if you asked right after breakfast, since you need to eat at mealtimes, and I'm sorry for that."

As I finished swallowing, Mommy hummed a tune and all the juice disappeared from my hands and face. I couldn't do that yet, but she kept telling me I'd be able to do magic one day. That was a fun one, too—always being clean; much easier to sneak around.

"What are all those papers for anyway?" I asked her, knowing she'd been looking at them for days.

"Something your daddy gave me that doesn't work like it should."

"Why?" I asked.

"He doesn't know."

"Do you know?"

"I have some thoughts, but I'm not sure."

"What is it then? Is he doing it wrong?" I squirmed in her grasp as she shifted me around.

"Mmm, I think he's built it right, but there's something else going on."

"Oh . . . what's it do?"

"It's a kind of special rock that thinks, and he wants it to do magic."

"Rocks don't think," I pointed out to her. "At least I don't think they do . . ."

"They don't, at least not any I've ever seen. That might be the problem, too. Not sure how to make a rock think."

"If they don't think, then how do you make them think?"

"Only living things think, Adia, not nonliving things like rocks or dirt."

"Then make it live?" I suggested.

"That's not easy to do, sweetie. I can't just make living things."

"You made me, though."

Mommy stopped, not moving at all, as she stared down at me and moved me back onto her hip. For a full count of sixty, which Daddy insisted was important for some reason, she looked at me.

"That's . . . not quite the same, sweetheart, but you're sort of right, aren't you?"

"Daddy helped," I told her. It's what they'd told me when I'd asked about where I came from.

She blushed a bit, giggling. "Yes he did, and I suppose he's already helped a lot here, too. I'll think about it."

"Thinking is good."

"Yes it is. You're pretty smart, too, Adia—a lot like your father."

"I'm not as silly," I replied, puffing out my cheeks.

"No, not nearly as silly. You've yet to knock holes in our home."

"Mmm." I nodded, seeing she had started to laugh again.

Today was a good day.

CHAPTER 13

DISAPPOINTMENT AND TEARS

Adia

I sighed as I looked around at all my friends, and our one open chair. Lunch was so long ago, so where was he? Daddy always came to see me for tea after lunch, always. Well, I guess sometimes he missed it, but if he did, he would tell me in the morning that he was going to, but he hadn't today. I was sure; so where was he?

Mad? Sad? I didn't know, but I was unhappy, and no matter how hard I tried, I still felt the frown pulling at my lips, pulling me down. There was even a tear trying to get out of my eye, but I wouldn't let it. I was big, I could handle being a little unhappy.

Just as I was pulling back a sniffle, the door flew open and there he was, standing and looking hurt.

"I'm so sorry, sweetie, I forgot to take my alarm with me."

"You weren't here!"

"No, I am late, and I am sorry, Adia," he said as he came and knelt beside me so I could look in his eyes. "I made a mistake. Everyone does sometimes, and while that's not a reason, it will happen. I can't promise that I will always be right, dear, but I will try. Can you forgive me?"

"You're supposed to be here for tea," I pouted, crossing my arms.

"As I said, I made a mistake. We all make mistakes sometimes." I saw him nod toward one of my toys, a stuffed doll, and tried to look away.

He'd given me that doll some time ago, and the next day I'd tripped, ripping its arm off when I fell on it. It hurt, and I was so sad, crying and trying to make it right. He didn't see it, though; nor did mommy. I'd hid it, not wanting them to see that I'd broken something brand new.

The next day at tea he asked where it was, since he knew I liked it, and he must have seen something, because he seemed to know something had happened. Daddy wasn't mad, though, and when he saw me crying again and saying I was sorry, he just smiled and patted my head. I could remember his words as he picked me up and carried me over to his chair. "It's okay, mistakes happen." That night he took me down to one of the workshops and fixed it while letting me sit on his lap.

I thought and thought, chewing on my lip.

"Okay, but you're supposed to be where you are supposed to be," I said after a time.

He leaned down and kissed my head before going back to where he normally sat and looked over at me.

"So, what is going on with you?" he asked as I poured some tea in his cup.

"Mommy is playing with rocks," I told him seriously, because well, she had been.

"Playing with rocks?" he asked a bit confused.

"Yes, playing with rocks. Normally, only you play with rocks."

He laughed for a moment. "Yes, I guess I do play with rocks a lot. Do you know why?" he asked.

"Because you are silly."

That made him laugh more, but he really shouldn't be. He was silly, and his silly was starting to get into other people. Uncle Chien was already too much like him, though also serious sometimes, and now he was getting to Mommy, too. That was no good, no good at all. How long until I, too, became full of nonsense, knocking holes in our house and playing with rocks. Actually, rocks were kind of cool, but no, no we couldn't have that. Someone had to make sure things were right.

"I suppose I am, but I do have reasons for it," he said after seeing my face.

"Mmm," I said, disagreeing as I pretended to drink my tea.

"It's strong today," he said after another sip.

"You're late."

"True. Well, I'll have to ask your mother why she's off playing with rocks, myself. Is there anything else going on?"

We talked for a while, a good long while about this and that. I had so many things going on all day today. There was a bug that was playing on one of the windows, and one of the workers was doing something loud while trying to move some equipment, and all kinds of things. Eventually, though, Daddy had to go.

That afternoon I went out into one of the courtyards. A couple of the people who worked here had kids, too, and today we were going to play. There was Oa, who was older, almost an adult since she was like thirteen, and then there was Lio, who was about my age. Oa mostly ignored us, instead playing other games by herself, only looking over every now and then to see what we were doing.

Lio and I played tag, a game Dad had taught me, and it was fun running around. We went back and forth across the courtyard, trying to get Oa to join us, but she didn't want to, not even bothering to tag one of us when she was 'it' and instead telling us to go away.

While we were running around, Lio fell on a loose rock and smacked his head on the ground. He was crying, and Oa was up immediately and running toward us.

"What happened? Are you okay!?" she asked, looking at me, even though I wasn't hurt. "If you're hurt, Mom will be so mad."

"It's Lio!" I told her, pulling away and going back to him.

"I fell!" he bawled, sitting up, red flowing down his face.

"We need to get someone," Oa said. "That's a lot of blood. Adia, stay here, don't move."

"It's gonna be okay, Lio," I told him, knowing that Mommy could patch that up in a second, even if nobody else could.

He had a big cut on his head and it was pouring out blood, making him scared and cry. It would be fine, though. I knew it would be fine, and I wanted him to feel better, not to hurt.

"I didn't mean to," he said through the tears.

"We all make mistakes," I told him, putting a hand on his shoulder, just wishing his cut would go away.

The world seemed to pulse with a bright glow I'd never seen before, and I felt things moving. His head was hurt and it shouldn't be; it wasn't right that it was. No, it was right for it to be better, for it not to hurt, for it not to bleed, or anything like that. As I thought that, as I put my hand on his shoulder, it felt like there was a light in my arm, a light that moved into him and right up to his head.

His big cut started to shift, to fill in with skin, to stop bleeding, and in a second, it looked like it just went away, like it had never been there in the first place. I blinked at the weird sight. Who had done that? In that moment, I felt so tired, so sleepy.

"It'll be okay. It'll be okay," I said. "I'm gonna lay down now." I curled up on the ground, sleep taking me like I'd tried to stay up late.

CHAPTER 14

A WORRIED MOTHER

Isha

Thankfully, Adia was all right. Finding her out cold on the ground had nearly made me faint. However, she was merely asleep, unlike her friend, who was crying up a storm. A quick once-over had shown that he was the one covered in blood, not her.

"I was playing, and running, and I fell, and . . ." he trailed off with a sob, thinking she was hurt or that we were angry.

"Calm," I told him, looking around at his head. "Where are you hurt?"

It was clear he had been the injured one. Perhaps the blood had simply scared little Adia that bad. So, I would attend to her in a moment. Now, though, I needed to fix whatever had happened.

"Here," he said, pointing to an uninjured spot on his head. "But it doesn't hurt anymore."

I looked between him and my daughter, him and my daughter again, and I understood.

“We're going to get someone to help you go wash up while I take care of Adia, okay?”

“Okay,” he said, sniffling.

I gathered my girl up in my arms, looking at her closely. It was there. I'd just missed it before because of how weak it was. She had an aura, a full proper aura, and while it was barely there now, it meant that she could cast. I'd been watching her for a while now, having seen one or two little flares here or there, having witnessed as she seemed to almost do a bit of magic, but now it was official.

After a few more words to get things going, I began to walk back toward the house.

“Are they okay, Miss Isha?” Oa asked as I neared the door. She, too, was worried.

“They'll be fine,” I told her. “You did good running to get an adult.” It was good to reinforce that behavior.

“Yes ma'am.”

Once Adia was cleaned up a bit and put on her bed, I waited, worrying. Back in our village, both Justin and I had been taken away for training. Old Elaya had made sure we were far away from other people while we learned to use our powers. Would we need to do that now? Send someone off with her for a few days? I didn't like the idea of sending my child away like that. The oldest elder there had insisted it was important, but I knew not everyone did such things here.

Perhaps Justin or I could do it instead, but that brought old arguments to mind. Parents could sometimes be poor at judging their children, and I knew both Justin and I fell into that category. He spoiled Adia too much, and if I were truthful, I didn't know if I'd be able to keep her away from people like that.

There were precious few I'd trust with her safety, either. Even here I was never too far away, ready to help her should something go wrong. There was that one old healer living at the cave, but she was brutal, and so far away. Even if we'd met a few times, I knew she'd not hurt a child, but who else? I couldn't trust any of the elders in the city. They were all too political for my liking. Rolan? No, he was an ancient and had far better things to do than look after a child for a few days, even if he was trustworthy. There was one other option . . .

"Mommy?" I heard from beside me.

"Oh, you're awake. How do you feel?" I asked, smiling at Adia.

"Heavy," she grumbled, before bolting upright. "Wait, you need to heal—"

"He's fine, Adia. Tell me what happened, and don't leave anything out."

"Well . . ." She wove her story, and though it was interrupted by the babbling that every child her age was likely to get into, she didn't lie, at least not so far as I could tell.

Her first spell and I'd missed it. I was a bit peeved about that, but it wasn't too odd. Magic tended to come when it was needed—under stress—and seeing that little boy, Lio, bleeding everywhere surely would have been stressful. That it was healing was both gratifying and concerning. Those with magic of that type could be magnificently powerful—helpful to all those around them, but they could also become terrors if they wanted.

"Are you mad?" she asked.

"No, sweetie, not at all. You didn't do anything wrong. In fact this is a very good day, but you're younger than I thought it would come."

"And that's bad?"

"No, it just makes things different. We'll have to talk to your father tonight."

"I'm not in trouble?"

"You aren't, though we'll have to go through some things, and it may feel like we're punishing you, but we aren't. You see, you're like me and your daddy, and you need to control that. The power in you can be very dangerous if you're not careful, you see, and you could hurt someone without meaning to."

"I don't want to hurt anyone."

"I know, but so that you don't, you may need to spend some time away from people learning. Both your father and I did the same, but I'll try to make it a bit better for you than we had it. It's not fun, not at all, but it is important."

"Okay," she said with the adorable seriousness children sometimes had.

Taking her hands and kissing her on the forehead, I pulled her into my lap.

"For now though you'll have to spend the day with me, and I don't want you trying, or wishing, or pushing on anything to make it do things, okay?"

"What do you mean?"

"Your magic is still young, and you've not learned to use it yet, so it's hard to explain, but just try to relax and not to change anything around you more than you need to."

"I don't really understand," she explained with a pout.

"That's okay."

CHAPTER 15

GETTING A TUTOR

Isha

"Whatever we choose, she needs training," I informed my husband after we'd put our child to bed. There were things you simply didn't need to discuss in front of them.

"Yes . . . I could."

"Justin, you spoil her more than you would ever admit. I know you love her, but she needs someone who can discipline her properly."

"So, you?" he asked, not denying it at all, merely offering another solution.

"I'm unsure," I replied. "What about finding someone professional?"

"I may know a few people," he said while tapping his lip in thought.

"Your apprentice, love. He's already like a member of the family, but you know he won't let her off the hook."

"Are we sure we want to keep up this tradition, anyway? We could train her together, with others. It wouldn't be so hard . . ."

"Justin, there's a reason for it. I know you hated it, and I did, too, but there was a good reason that old bitch made us all go out into the wilderness. You know what kind of power we can wield; you know what abilities can come from it. What if she hurts someone, even unintentionally, or kills them?"

"It's true. Did you know that I saw what Jina did during the war? What she was capable of."

He didn't talk about that much. That battle had been horrible, and while everyone remembered it, and even he would use it if he had to, he didn't like to, and in our private time we rarely spoke about that chapter of our lives.

"I know she did something, killed all those children . . ."

"It was instant. I doubt our little girl could do that right now, but one day she might be able to. We need to keep her from going down that path. I shudder to think what could happen should she do so one day."

"Do you think she'd pose a danger to us now?" I asked.

"No, not as we are. Our power would push hers aside, but other children, possibly."

That was something he'd told me about seeing first in the southern swamps. One of the soldiers there had been able to resist spells, and after some inquiries, and a bit of practice, both us and Chien could now do the same. It was an odd technique, but very useful. I suspected that most of the elders knew of it, and it's probably why old Elaya had insisted in taking the children to train herself.

"Chien will be the best for it then," I insisted. "He's a decent man."

"He's a bit of a joker," my husband replied.

"Only about things that are fine to joke about. You've seen how he is when things are bad, or serious. You also trust him, and so do I."

"Fine then. If you're sure, I'll speak to him tomorrow morning," he offered.

"No, I'll do it. Need to make sure he knows how seriously I take this," I said clicking my tongue a few times. "He sees you and still thinks you're about fun."

"Generally speaking, he's right, too." He settled beside me, and we headed to bed, both tired from the long day.

The next morning I found our long-time friend and my husband's apprentice.

"Whatever it is, I didn't do it," he said as I came to his section of our compound.

He was no longer a boy, which was sort of sad. Having known him as such, it was a bit nostalgic. However, he still acted like one enough, chasing women, making jokes, and not taking many things seriously at all.

"It's not what you did, it's what I want you to do," I told him simply.

"And what's that?"

"I want you to train Adia in basic magic."

"That seems like a horrible idea. Why would I do that?" he asked with a scoff, and then I heard something fall nearby. He saw me look around and simply said, "Don't worry about it."

"Because you're the best man for the job."

"That seems inaccurate, and anyway, the boss needs me for his current projects."

"I assure you he doesn't, and he agrees with me. He trusts you, Chien. He knows that you'll keep her safe, that you'll see to it that she learns what she needs to. Do you know how many people he trusts? So few that the best candidates for this job are in this room. Well, there may be a few more, but not that we can contact."

"She's your child, and from what I've heard, her magic is more like yours anyway. Rumor is she healed that boy. Yes, there it is, and it's true. I can see it on your face. You know, and I know that I know nothing about raising kids—don't want to, don't need to."

"You remember our trip with Rolan?" I asked him.

"The ancient from the forests to the north? Sure, what about it?"

"You yourself claimed to be raised by my husband, and while I personally think he views you more like a little brother, he needs your help now, regardless. You're still Chien, of the tree of Justin, aren't you? Will you let his child have something subpar and potentially dangerous just to spare yourself some discomfort?"

"You're a real monster, Isha. You know that?"

"And by that you mean I'm right?" I pointed out.

"Fine, but you're spending the day here teaching me what I need to know." As he spoke, the door to his personal bedroom opened, a small face peeking out curiously, skin peeking through the cracked portal. "Er, one moment, need to see to this first, though."

I spent very few thoughts on if I'd made the right choice as he spoke with his previous night's companion. She worked here, at least, which meant that she wasn't a security risk, but still thinking that this was the man I was handing my child over to bothered me deeply.

"All right, let's begin with everything you think I should know," he finally said as he returned, looking at me with a crooked smile.

CHAPTER 16

✧

BEGINNING INSTRUCTION

Chien

I looked at the child and her small satchel.

"So . . . you have everything you need?" I asked.

"Mommy helped me pack it; said not to bring much, though," she complained.

"We won't need much; mostly we're going to be doing magic." There was no need to hide that from her.

"You're actually going to teach me? Mommy just told me to be careful and not do it right now."

"Yes, and she was right to," I said, leaning down to her level. I remembered how I'd hated being talked down to when I was smaller. "Our powers are pretty dangerous if we're not careful, and she doesn't want you to hurt yourself, or anyone else."

"I don't wanna hurt anyone, Uncle Chien."

"I know, kid, I know, but don't worry. We'll go out for a bit, and once you've got some basics, we'll come back. Easy as that."

"Will it really be that easy?" she asked.

"Well, it'll probably take a couple of weeks, and you probably won't like it all that much, but it'll be fine. Just remember why you're doing it. That's what I do when I have to do things I don't like."

"You do things you don't like?" My, she asked a lot of questions.

"All the time; everyone does. Sometimes I don't like the job I need to do, but I know what comes from it when I do it, so I do it anyway. This is like that."

Her parents had already said their goodbyes and the two of us waited to leave. We were going under cover of darkness. Justin had suggested it, and I wholeheartedly agreed. It would be better if fewer people knew we were leaving and where we were going. He had enemies, after all, and there was no reason to let them know his child would be away from his compound.

So, the two of us waited for a bit while the darkness got deeper, the moon was new, and my oldest friend had arranged for someone to sing clouds and fog into the sky. Once things were in place, I scooped up little Adia in my arms and we soared into the air.

Flying was, at its absolute best, a mana-heavy and slightly uncomfortable way to move. There'd been a lot of kinks to this spell that Justin and I had once tackled, but it still kind of sucked as a long-distance method of travel. He'd shown me his first version some time ago—the one he used for scouting while we traveled the world—and that was a hundred times worse than what I had access to now, but even this was subpar compared to just walking. After all, it was just a little slower and much easier overall. He seemed to think his flying platforms would be much better, though, so that might have potential.

We didn't go far, just outside the city with a view from the walls before we landed.

"I don't like that," Adia complained.

"Me neither, but it worked."

"Boo."

We spoke little on our way to our temporary home—an old, abandoned quarry surrounded by fruit trees. The quarry itself was ours, long used for getting the limestone for making cement, a popular product. However, getting the stone out here had become progressively harder over the years, so we'd eventually let it go downhill. Now there was nothing but a large, water-filled hole surrounded by trees, which had been some of our earlier attempts at farming. They'd been only a marginal success but were still pretty.

I got Adia to wait on a pile of dirt while I began to build. My magic was strong, almost at the level of an elder myself, and ripping a few large stones from the side and forming them into a small but livable house was the work of only a few minutes. With all the ingredients I needed, I even formed rudimentary cement, locking them all in place one by one. There were small bedrooms for me and Adia, a central space for a little fire, and a sturdy roof.

By the time I turned back to her, she'd fallen asleep. We were well past her normal bedtime, so that was understandable. Carefully picking her up, I got her to her sleeping room and began to do a bit more setup. If I was going to be here for a few weeks, it could at least be decent.

"Ah, you're awake," I said as she stumbled out of her room the next morning.

"You woke up before me," she observed.

"Not quite," I said. "I slept before we left and will sleep again tonight, but don't worry about that. Are you ready to begin?" My question perked her right up.

"Yes! What are we doing? Healing things? Making another house?"

"Not quite; we're starting small." I pointed to a small vine, a clipping I'd put in a little pot of dirt. "See if you can make that grow."

"But . . ."

"One step at a time, Adia. If you can make a plant grow a little, we can move on to bigger and better things. First, though, we need to start with something that won't hurt anyone should it die."

The plant died. Poor thing never stood a chance. Adia had a little bit of power—about the right amount for her age—but she pushed it too hard.

"Grow the roots first, and monitor its condition as you go. You should be able to feel how it is doing if you make a spell to do it, and for things like big injuries you'll need to," I advised, knowing at least the basics of healing from my prep for this excursion.

It was slow going, but that was okay. Ideal, even. Small wounds could be healed and repaired with no problem, but major ones had to be done in phases; everyone knew that. If you tried to regrow a hand all in one go, you were likely to make someone extremely sick, and a full limb could drain their body dry, potentially killing the patient. Slow was good, slow was safe, and I told her all of this as she slowly worked on vine after vine. Luckily, the things grew everywhere here, so there was no shortage of supply.

We took breaks for some fruit and dried meats, and by the end of the day she could coax a good bit of growth from them, and even shape them to an extent. That was when I assigned her, her first actual job—growing us decent beds. I threw up a couple of frames from a mixture of stone and wooden supports and led her through weaving vines into mattresses. By the end of it, she fell into hers and was instantly asleep.

I went to mine shortly after, enjoying the soft bounce of the plants, which I'd surely not planned out, wanting to sleep well rather than spend a night on the hard dirt. With that thought in my head, I chuckled, drifting off to dream.

CHAPTER 17

GETTING THE BASICS DOWN

Chien

It took us a few weeks to get deep into the subject of magic, but it was fun. I got to teach little Adia not only what I knew about her powers but also what I knew about the wilds. Perhaps I was no master woodsman, but over the years I'd at least learned a fair amount about how to live out here, like what plants were edible and where to find them.

"I can't believe you didn't know any of this. Even I knew some of this at your age," I said as I shook my head one day.

"Daddy doesn't let me into the woods often," she replied with a pout.

"Suppose he doesn't, does he. Well, no time like now to learn."

"Did you spend much time in the woods when you were my age, Uncle Chien?" she asked.

"No, mostly in the city, but I did have to come out every now and then for things, so I learned a little bit."

"Were you a farmer?"

"Haha, no, farming wasn't really much back then, either. People would go out in groups to get food. Some still do, but a lot of people have realized that getting the plants to grow where you want them is easier. Things were . . . very different then."

I thought back on the slaves that we'd had, well, still had. There weren't as many now, as with the advent of scaled farming, one magic user could do much more than hundreds of gatherers could in a day, but some people still had them for helping on the farms. At least it was safer, as you could manage the land a lot more carefully than someone going out to new places every day. More people in the same place, more power to bring down on any monster or beast that attacked.

"You must be old, huh?"

"Pfft, not that old. Things have changed a lot, really a lot in the last few decades. Justin brought so many changes."

"Do you like them?"

"Sometimes, sometimes not, but I think that's the way of things."

"You know, Mommy says you're a mess, but you seem pretty smart, Uncle Chien."

"Ha! Well, sometimes I am, but I have a way I do things. I think that's important."

"What do you mean?"

"I mean that I do get into troublesome situations sometimes, but I still do things the way I think is right. Your mother doesn't like all the girls I bring around, but I don't lie to them, I don't do anything they're not fine with, and I don't promise anything I won't deliver. Try to do the same in business, too. Maybe I'm not nice to people, but I'm honest with them. Things work out better that way."

"Honesty is good. You shouldn't lie to people."

"No, indeed not, but you also have to keep a code for yourself, and hold yourself to it. Decide the way you want to act, and then act that way. Maybe it'll change a bit over time, but it shouldn't be a problem. We learn as we grow, after all, so changes are fine, but it's important to have rules for yourself that you follow, not because you have to, but because you want to."

That put her into deep thought—not a bad thing at all—and gave me a few moments to myself.

If I were being honest with myself, I knew I was a bit of a lecher, but what I'd told her was true. I didn't make promises to women I wouldn't keep, never led them on; though, some did still think I did. Nor did I ever try to hurt them. It was just that I liked girls. They were just fun, but none I wanted to spend the rest of my life around. I just couldn't really bond to them like Justin did with Isha. Maybe one day that would change; maybe not, but it was the way it was. To me, they were all just fun. That was all I wanted, and all I wanted them to know they'd get from me.

"That was a smart thing to say, Uncle Chien," Adia said after a long while, pulling me from my thoughts.

"Why, thank you," I joked.

"I think I need to think about it a lot."

"Take your time, kiddo. Sometimes we need to plan before we do, and now is a great time for that."

I gave her hours to work on it, mumbling to herself and writing a few things in the dirt. It was odd how she'd taken to that little thing, making notes in the dirt or on bits of bark for herself. Not something I really did, but it's not like it hurt anything.

Over our time here, we'd covered most of the basics. She worked mostly on plants at first, but in time, I'd had to catch a few animals, giving them minor injuries for her to fix. It had also been a good time for her to practice sedating them, something she was now very capable of.

Of course, attack magic was something she needed, too, but it was not a subject in which my student excelled. For me, it had been easy. Fire, or water or, like Justin often preferred, pure force—all of those and many others worked. However, healers were different; they had very different options.

Knocking out animals that weren't at all magical was one thing, but against an actual attacker, it wouldn't do. Adia wasn't powerful enough to affect anything with even a bit of an aura without real effort, and in combat, failing to achieve anything could be deadly. So, I had to instruct her on how to harm with her powers.

She'd only ever used that spell against plants, never animals, and it was a nasty thing. I'd seen them before, of course—magics that rotted flesh, and it was a monster of something to hit someone with. However, that didn't change the fact that she needed to be able to defend herself—no arguments—and so, we'd have to consider her lack of experience.

That wouldn't do; no, not at all. It wasn't nice, but she needed to see what her magic could do, needed to know it on a visceral level.

We'd have to hunt something together so that she knew it would be all right. Once that was done, once I was sure she could defend herself and not go wild when she did, we'd be done here. With a satisfied smile I laid back, readying for that final test.

CHAPTER 18

FINAL TEST

Adia

Uncle Chien and I slipped through the underbrush, him pointing every now and then at tracks or something. Some of it I could see, but most of it, I had no clue what he was talking about.

"See here, look at the way the hoof splits, and it's not too big. This is what we should be after."

"But it looks deep," I complained. "You said deep means it's big."

He smiled. "Deep means heavy. These are all heavy, but don't worry—if it's too much I'll be here."

"Okay . . ."

I kept moving, just like he'd shown me, keeping quiet, keeping to the shadows. Uncle Chien was really good at sneaking—better than me even—and the things he'd taught me here would be great for later. When we finally got home, I'd be even more of a shadow than I already was.

The tracks went along a path, one I could see through the trees.

It looked like something had been past here again and again, leaving a blank spot. I quietly called out to Uncle Chien.

"How do we know these aren't old?" I asked. "If it came through here a lot."

"Oh, good question, but when did it last rain?" he asked.

"Two days ago?" I said after thinking a bit.

"Last night."

"I didn't hear it . . ."

"No, you'd gone to bed. Look at the edges of the tracks; they're fresh, very fresh."

"You're good at this, huh?" I said.

"No, Adia, I'm not. I only know a few things. If I were good, we'd have found something much easier to go after."

That couldn't be right. He knew where the creature was that we were after. He knew how to find it. He even knew the weather I'd not noticed. If he wasn't good, then I didn't know what good was.

"You've hunted, though."

"With your father when I was younger. We traveled and had to get food, but less about that now. I think we're getting closer."

With a nod I got quiet and we continued to follow the path. If he said we were getting closer, we must be, and I didn't want to spook the prey. It took time—things always took time, sadly—but soon enough we found a clearing.

Slowly, I began to move around it, looking for any more prints or the animal we were after. I didn't want to go out into the opening because I'd been told that a lot of animals could see or hear better than I could.

But there were no other tracks, and I didn't see any animals. Confused, I looked at Uncle Chien, shrugging. With a slight smile and a shake of his head he pointed, right to the middle of the field.

There were no animals in the middle of the field. I looked and looked, but nothing. All there was, was grass and a big rock. I squinted, and almost went into the open area, but Uncle Chien held me back, pointing again at the rock. Now I had no choice but to wait. I couldn't talk right now or we might scare the animal, but I just didn't see it.

While I waited I prepared a spell, forming it in my hands. This animal was supposed to be a bit dangerous, not too bad, but something we shouldn't let roam close to the city, so it was good to stop it. I'd been told that those like us had responsibilities to protect people without magic, and that made sense. The spell I made wasn't supposed to rot like some of the others I'd been shown before, but just make things stop. It would make the animal die quickly, painlessly; that was the better way to do it.

Time passed, but I still didn't see it. I was nearly ready to ask if Uncle Chien was playing with me when the rock stood up. The rock was the monster, and I'd missed it. It had four stubby legs, and an almost-cute face, with a flat nose and two . . . big teeth, one on either side. After standing, it went to munch on the grass, which was weird, because grass tastes horrible.

I gasped in surprise, and the beast turned, eyes shifting over us before locking onto me. It let loose a loud roar, and I pushed my magic forward, slamming into it like a ball I'd thrown. I hit one of the legs, and even though that should have been enough to stop it, the creature just stumbled then charged.

As quickly as I could, I formed another spell, then another, eventually giving up on this one and just making the rotting one. I threw them as fast as I could, as it tried to get up and run toward us, each hit making it flinch or turn. It didn't stop, though. It just kept coming.

Before I realized it, the rock thing had gotten close, really close. It would be on us any second. I kept trying to hit it, kept trying to stop it, but couldn't. It wouldn't die. Panic crept up my back, and I felt tears in my eyes. Why had we done this? Why hadn't I brought more help?

Then a blue lance slammed into the creature's mouth, throwing it back and onto its butt.

"Don't stop; it's not dead," Uncle Chien said as I continued to pour magic into the struggling beast.

Another few moments, and it stopped moving, but I kept hitting it just to make sure.

"That's enough, Adia," he said to me calmly, putting a hand on my shoulder.

I breathed, shaking.

"I don't . . . It didn't . . ."

"I know, kiddo. Maybe we should have started with something a bit weaker . . . Thought you could deal with this one, but maybe I'm getting a bit skewed in my old age. Sorry for that, but you did a good job, and a good thing."

"A good thing?! I killed it, it wasn't doing anything, and I killed it!"

"Adia, you saw how it reacted to seeing us. What if you and I didn't have magic, hmm? How would one of your friends have dealt with that? Maybe you don't like killing—and that's good; you shouldn't—but sometimes you have to do things you don't like to help others."

I breathed deep for a few moments, letting him talk.

"I don't wanna do that again," I complained.

"Well, good news. With what you've done here, I'm happy to say you're ready to go home. How does seeing your mom and dad again sound?" he asked.

"Good . . ." I mumbled.

"Then, let's go home, kid." He ruffled my hair, and I had to spend a moment getting it back to normal again, poofing out my cheeks to show him how much I disliked him doing that.

CHAPTER 19

ADIA COMES HOME

It had been too long for me, but finally my child was back. Well, I guess Chien was back, too, but he could take care of himself.

"Adia!" I called, scooping her up as she ran to me.

They'd just gotten back into town, and luckily, I'd been home to meet them. Adia was crying, going on and on in gibberish. I tried but, sadly, failed to understand. Rather than try to fight it, I let her go, keeping her close and trying to calm her down. From what I gathered, she was just happy to be home.

"Did anything bad happen?" I asked when she'd finally relaxed.

"There was a monster, and I fought it, and I didn't like it, and I don't want to again, and it was scary, and I don't really like being out of the city," she told me, letting her sentence run on and on for a while.

"What about good things?" I asked.

"Uncle Chien showed me how to use magic, and it was fun," she finally said before burying herself in my chest again. "Can we go see Mommy?"

"Of course." I gave a nod to Chien, who just smiled and shook his head.

My long-time friend made some noises about bathing and meandered off as I took Adia to go see Isha. It was why I'd been home right now, anyway, so it was perfect timing. Soon enough, we found her mother, who experienced the same greeting I had. Our child all but ran to her and rolled up in her arms.

"You need a wash," Isha said.

"Mmm," Adia agreed.

"Why don't you two take care of that while I go see about getting us some food?" I offered.

"Sounds good," Isha said as she carried Adia off to the washroom. "Come now, let's get clean while Daddy gets something to eat."

"Meet me in the kitchen!" I called as the door closed, smiling the whole way.

By the time I got there, I met my assistant, his hair still wet. It looked like he'd gone and scrubbed himself quickly before heading the same direction I was.

"You hungry, too?" I asked.

"I don't mind camping food, but it's just not the same. Personally, I've never been a good cook, and without tons of ingredients . . ."

"No need to explain, I get it."

My compound was massive, and we always had something going. Normally, it was soup or stew of some form, something anyone could come and get if they needed a meal. Even more, currently, being as it was right about lunchtime. There were a few dedicated cooks, and one waved from beside a small spit over a fire. There was a great smell coming from it.

"What do we have today?" I asked with a smile.

"Roasted deer; added some fat from other animals and sauce. Also have some cooked fruits and veggies if you want some," the girl offered with a smile.

It all looked mouth-watering, the meat glistening as she slowly rotated it, the fat and juices barely coming to the surface. It wasn't quite the same as food from back on Earth, as there were still a lot of ingredients we just didn't have, but it was quite good, and as far as I could tell, pretty healthy, too.

"Three plates," I told her, as Chien and I found our preferred spot off to the side, away from where others would be.

"How are things going here? All well?" he asked.

"Quite so. I got a lot done, actually."

I hated to admit it, but having Adia away for a while meant I spent much more time getting things done. My time with her was the highlight of my days, but they were also a massive interruption; and even if I wouldn't trade them for the world, not having the interruptions for a few weeks enabled me to throw myself at my project with a frenzy. Honestly, I'd hoped to be done by the time she got home, but we had no such luck.

"So you ready to launch your little flying thing?" he asked.

"Sadly, no, though it's close. I've still got a few last touches to put on—proper cargo areas, some of the weapons that aren't all the way on yet; that kind of thing. We may need to rush it, though."

"Why?" he asked.

"Got word the other day," I said. "Looks like Rolan is trying to get people together for something. I'm not sure on the details, but it seems he's sent messengers to all the major regions—fast ones."

"To what end?" Chien asked.

"Right now? It appears he's trying to gather information on our new western neighbors, but I suspect that is just the first step."

Rolan was an ancient who lived to the north of us, ruled it truly, and not someone I'd want to cross. Most regions had been ruled by elves like him, well over a thousand years old and powerful beyond what most of us could imagine, but several had been lost in the last century. Now I knew of only two true ancients, and among them he seemed the most powerful.

"I'd give him good odds on killing anything if he puts his mind to it," Chien put forth.

"Same, but if he's calling for people to let him know what they know, there may be more to it than we've yet seen. I don't know about you, but if he seems concerned, it may be we should be as well."

"So more and bigger weapons?"

"It's like you're reading my mind," I said with a smile. "Though we'll need to act carefully. Don't want the council to get spooked and do something foolish."

"The council, do something stupid? Whoever heard of such a thing?" His sarcasm made me smile.

CHAPTER 20

BLIMP

We walked through the workshop, Chien's eyes drawn up to the blimp above us.

"It's massive," he said under his breath.

"Not really. No, a full one should be several times this size."

"For what possible fucking reason?" he asked.

"Moving across landscapes full of explosives," I informed him.

My blimp was still massive by any scale, but really they all were. I was also pushing what I knew more than a bit, since I'd never actually been on one before. These things weren't exactly common in my day and age, with only a few still in service anywhere in the world. Turned out planes were a lot better by basically every metric for almost every case. Then again, I was also pretty sure I couldn't make one of those, so blimps it was.

Filling the thing with helium had been a chore, as I'd had to create a spell to make the stuff myself, and that was not at all easy. For some reason, magic didn't really like doing fusion, and it had taken quite a bit of time and effort to make it happen. That seemed odd to me, but there were decidedly some underlying rules somewhere that I'd not quite sussed out yet. Even after I'd managed to get the spell to make helium, it still hadn't produced any energy at all; odd since I'd really worried about that possibility.

"Planning to erase forests?" Chien asked.

"If we need to, but I surely hope not."

"With enough of your crystals we definitely could . . ."

"We're not using those, either—too powerful, too dangerous. I've been working on bombs, though, things like I used in the war, only a lot less nasty; well, most of them are less nasty."

I'd prepared some good old-fashioned powder bombs—simple, easy to understand, nontoxic. This contrasted with what I'd used against Cino when he'd come to our city to raze it, and while I could still pull some of those things out if I needed them, things like chlorine trifluoride and chlorine gas would hopefully be overkill for anything we needed to fight again.

"The council might be alarmed if you brought those back out."

"The council can deal with it if I do. They're too concerned with what I'll do to defend this city and not nearly concerned enough with what they can do to defend it."

"I see the cannon, too. Just the one?"

"Limited amount of room for ammunition. We're actually quite under-armed."

"That I do not believe." Cheeky bastard.

"Come on, let's go in," I told him, with a sigh.

We got a small ladder into the cabin which, honestly, wasn't all that large—two little rooms and a pair of chairs. The controls were . . . well, manual. With levers that could be pulled and a system to light any bombs, it was, frankly, a bit embarrassing with all the magic I had at my disposal. I really would have liked something better, but better would be more complex, and harder to make, and even with all I'd done, I still hadn't perfected too much.

"Just the two?" Chien asked.

"Like I said, it's undersized. If my calculations are correct, we'll be able to stay up with two safely, but if we went too much heavier . . ."

"People don't weigh that much."

"No, but food, water, and the things they need do. This vehicle is made for a trip of over a week carrying as much ordinance as I could manage. If I brought even one more person, it would cut that amount of firepower down significantly."

"So only one other."

"Only one—you, I hope," I told him with a half-smile.

"Who else would you even choose, boss?" he joked.

"I don't know, some of the new recruits are doing pretty well . . ."

"And here I thought you were going to hold off on any adventures until Adia was grown," he said, shaking his head.

That made me frown. It had been my promise to my wife. After our last little disaster of a trip, I'd told her I'd be holding off on any adventures until our first child was fully grown, but could I? Would I have the time?

"Hopefully we'll not need it, or we'll just need to go within a day of the city. If we can manage that, I'll have kept my word."

"And if we can't?"

"I've spoken to Isha. She's not pleased with it, but if the reports are true, those things are a real threat to us. Again, we'll hold this for defensive actions just in case, but if we need to—really need to—she's given me her blessing to go."

"Seems a bit worried for some monsters, even if they are nasty."

"We've gotten more reports while you've been away. They're not public yet, but our current guess is that each of those creatures can fight an elder."

"Shit."

"Indeed. I think Rolan may be trying to organize something. We'll know more after his summit, but until then . . ."

"Until then we get as ready as we can. Honestly, I'm surprised they didn't try to get you to go to his summit."

"They did, but I managed to convince Shorin to volunteer. He's older than I am, and I need to finish this anyway, so it wasn't too hard."

"He should manage."

Shorin was an old . . . Friend may not have been the best word, but ally perhaps. He'd been here in Atal when I'd first arrived, grandfather to one of the guards I ended up knowing quite well, and he was here still. The man had more respect than I did, and more clout with the other elders due to his age, but I also liked him. Sure, he was out for himself, but he also looked after his family—a staple here in Atal—so I could trust that he would do the best he could.

"I hope he does."

CHAPTER 21

SUMMIT

Shorin

Three weeks I'd traveled which, in the long run, wasn't all that bad, but it was a horrid trip. Only a few of us had come, with a leaning toward speed. Several of my escorts were strong or fast enough to keep pace while I simply used my inner fire to push and pull myself at high speed.

Now we neared a massive tree, which just yesterday had been a speck poking out of the horizon. Guides were joining us, making sure that we didn't cause trouble or get lost, as if we could have missed the giant, whose owner we were going to see.

"Any word?" I asked one of the men who'd come to escort us.

"Not yet, but like I told you yesterday, the emissaries from both the north and the far south arrived yesterday."

"I'd love to know how those mud-caked bastards beat us here," I grumbled under my breath.

"Ask them when we get there, then," the escort retorted, loud enough for everyone to hear. These men were certainly skilled, if he could hear that from his current position.

We moved in silence, and I struggled to keep my face stony. Sure, I'd heard stories about these trees, but they were more than I'd ever expected. Each one was big enough to house several families, and I'm talking about the smaller ones; the larger ones might have more wood in them than resided in all of Atal. Even still, I saw some things we did better.

Their obsession with living in trees meant that their technology was hampered. After all, it was hard to make metal while surrounded by something that could burn. Their food also looked to be fresh, with almost everything I'd seen uncooked, like berries and nuts. That meant that they missed out on important sources of food, and a storable ones, too.

As night began to fall we made it to the base of the giant, a hanging basket ready to pull us up.

"What is that monstrosity?" I asked looking at the basket. It looked even worse than some of Justin's most egregious nonsense.

"For going up and down. Used to be a lot simpler looking, but the maker added all those extra ropes and whatnot to it. Claimed that it made it safer, but I'm not convinced."

Honestly, I wasn't convinced, either. If this was supposed to be "safer" I'd have hated to see what it was like before. When I got in, there were five woven ropes hooked onto different places, and the whole thing rocked enough to nearly make my stomach sick. It did make the trip go by faster than if I'd have done it on foot, though—something easy to notice as we quickly passed layer after layer of platforms, winding around the giant.

"Welcome, welcome," Rolan intoned as we entered his hall nearly an hour later, several elves much older than me sitting around a large table, a space for myself left conspicuously open. "For your representative," the ancient said with a wave. "When he arrives."

"I am the representative ancient," I informed him.

"Is that so? I was hoping to see that young one once more. Does he do well?" As he spoke, I saw the other two here perk up, looking at me with hard eyes.

"Justin is well, but unable to come for now."

"Why is that?" asked the female of the group, eyes settling on me like ice. Her skin was so pale, almost fragile looking.

"A mixture of things—labors and an agreement he made with his wife." My response drew a pair of snickers from her companions, our host's eyes gleaming with a smile.

"Fool boy," she said. I knew from reports that this was Matriarch Neera of the north, their leader and another true ancient. It wouldn't do well to cross her.

"Perhaps, but we have other concerns at the moment," Rolan said as he motioned me to sit. "I'm sure by now you've all heard the reports.

"Heard the reports?" Neera huffed. "We lost dozens from the villages we'd settled on the western coast. Whole villages were ravaged, their people made homeless and fleeing back to my hold."

"That's why we're here," I pointed out. "So we can coordinate. I'll admit to my shame that our city cannot field anyone equal to you, Ancient, nor you," I said with a nod to Rolan. "But we can provide some aid, and we will."

"It is appreciated," Rolan said, and the final member of the delegations, an elder much further along the path than myself, nodded to him, looking worried. "But what we need now is information, for it might make the difference between success and failure. I'll admit, I was too young the last time these beasts appeared to have done much, or even heard too much, but I think one of our number was much closer to the action."

"I was young," the matriarch began, sounding distant as we looked on. "Barely past my hundredth year when they came last. First was the wave of monsters, all beasts of note in their own right. They razed everything before them, leaving only a few of our groups standing. The ancients that lived then took action, one from the plains and the other from the mountains, falling upon those things. Those two hated each other, had warred for years, but they put their differences aside for that war. My own family was sent to flee north, to hide away from the fighting while they solved it, but I stayed behind.

"We cut through them like they were hardly there, but there were so many, and then we saw it. Their numbers were shrinking after the surge, but each one that fell, the others consumed, getting larger and stronger. Soon enough it was only elders or large groups of skilled fighters that could combat even the weakest of them. Then only large groups of elders. The cost in lives . . . My own people's numbers still haven't recovered.

"In the end there were only two, a male and female. Their size, their power, it was almost indescribable, like standing in a fire. The male fought the ancients of that era and won, but through their sacrifice, and that of over a dozen elders, we managed to slay the beast. They'd led him to the north, and where his body fell, a fissure was created that remains even today.

"I was all that was left, the last of the force that had gone to kill them. So I went for the female, not sure what I could do, if I could do anything."

"Stories tell that you slew the beast," I observed, having heard of the tale once or twice in my time.

"Stories are just that," she said coldly. "It was in one of the burning mountains, far up the side, and the female was in the process of dying when I found it. The creature's burning blood was everywhere, covering the whole cliff it had settled on. I didn't even strike the last blow, too afraid to get near it."

"So you didn't kill it?" Uro asked. "Just claimed you did?"

"Think me a coward if you like; it is true enough. No, I butchered the beast after it fell, taking its heart to build Icehome for what remained of my people." Had her hair not been purest white, I'd have thought her a child with how her voice sounded, small, scared, tired.

"So how do we kill them?" Rolan asked.

"I haven't the slightest idea what we could do. My magic is weaker than the previous warriors who fought them, and we have only the two of us that could perhaps do it. I'd hoped the boy Justin might be of use."

Rolan looked at me expectantly. "He's made some potent weapons in the past," I observed.

"We need to contact him; I fear we'll need everything we can get."

"More of what he used to kill Nora, perhaps," Uro mused.

What in the world was he talking about? I'd have to ask my irksome ally.

CHAPTER 22

MESSAGES

Shorin's message had been short and disturbing.

"Prepare weapons to fight ancient-level opponents. Come as soon as you're ready." Such things never bode well for anyone, much less whole societies.

"There's got to be more than that," I told the messenger as he stood at attention.

"No, that was all he said."

"I have problems with this," Chien piped up from a corner.

"Agreed," I told him. "Tell me what else you know," I said to the messenger.

"That isn't my job," he said with a turn, heading toward the door to my meeting room.

The door was quickly blocked by a wall of force between him and me. I might have enough magical ability to toss out complex force constructs casually, but I didn't want to get punched by someone fast enough to cross that distance quickly.

"I wasn't asking," I told him as he turned and jolted toward me, slamming into the other wall there. "And allow me to be clear, I am an elder, responsible for making weapons that, as you have recently told me, are to be made for ancient-level enemies. You will tell me what I'm dealing with to the best of your knowledge."

Pushing too often wasn't my style, and would make me a lot of enemies, but there were times that I needed to. Times when disrespect couldn't be tolerated for a number of reasons, and this was certainly one of them. The man began to spit insults and yell, and in response, I shrunk the box he was in. I'd long mastered the use of kinetic fields, and this was no different.

"Wait! STOP!" he finally yelled when he was in a space about the size of a coffin. "You cannot do this; my leader will destroy you."

"Your leader? Rolan, right? We've met, and I assure you, he won't. Be angry? Well, perhaps. Disappointed? Certainly. But, destroy me? No chance." Chien snickered. "So are you going to tell me what I want to know, or am I going to see what happens when you crush someone between planes of magic?"

"I-I don't know much, I swear! The message I was given was it. They didn't tell me any of the details about what they wanted!"

"Who all was there, and their disposition with each other?" I asked.

He rambled off descriptions I recognized, and that quickly told me what I needed to know—both of the extant ancients were there, along with Uro, somehow, and Shorin, our own representative. They also weren't fighting or arguing as such, though they all seemed to have locked themselves away in deep discussion.

The man hadn't tried to hide anything from me; he just didn't want to look a fool. Well, that ship had sailed.

"Go," I finally told him as I released him from the tiny little prison.

"I will tell Rolan of this," he threatened, poofing up like an angry bird.

"Please do, do tell him that you came to me, telling me to make and bring along incredibly powerful weapons to his home without any further information. I'm sure he'll be thrilled with that."

The man huffed uselessly once more before turning and leaving at speed. I'd have to check to make sure he actually left later, but that could wait. Not that I really expected him to retaliate; he was a messenger, and I was, on some level, his client. He'd be pissy for a while, but people like him didn't come to stab you in the middle of the night.

We sat in relative silence for a few minutes while I thought of all the things I could take, all the places I could put weapons, and what ones would be best to bring. Reports said that our enemy used fire, so fire would probably not be the best thing to take along. My cannon was, of course, coming, and the hammer I'd remade. To that I could add some of the nastier poisons, though that might be amiss. Cold would be ideal, but it wasn't something I had anything for at the moment; nor could I make crystallized magic for it at a rate that would be even a little helpful.

"I dislike this," I said with a frown.

"You can say that again," Chien agreed.

"I dislike this."

"But you're going to do it anyway?" he asked.

"Yes. Shorin isn't a fool, nor is Rolan, for whom that man decidedly works. If they want me to bring all of my nastiest toys to the play area, then something has gone quite wrong." There weren't playgrounds in this world yet, so I had to mangle what I actually wanted to say, something which still grated on me from time to time.

"You think those monsters are that much of a threat, though?"

"I think they think they are. Doesn't hurt to be prepared at any rate, though, just in case they're right."

"We have some of that stuff boss, the stuff you keep pushed to the back, but not much of it."

"No, we'll spend a week making what we can, then we head out."

"Sounded like they wanted us there fast."

"Slow is smooth, smooth is fast," I mused, remembering something I'd heard from a military man on my previous world once.

"Not sure that applies here, boss, but better to have it and not need it, than need it and not have it, right?"

"You're picking things up."

"Been picking things up from you forever."

After informing the proper parties about our guest and how he needed to be kept an eye out for, we laughed and headed to work. Sure, I didn't believe he would come back for something stupid, but if he did, he wouldn't leave again. My family lived here, after all, and I wouldn't be tolerating anything threatening them, even a little.

CHAPTER 23

ROAD TRIP

"Weapons?"

"Secured."

"The doors are open; time to do this," I intoned, nervous chills running through my body.

Today was the first day people on this world would fly via machine. Sure, some powerful spellcasters like myself could, but this would be something else, something anyone would be able to use in time. We were ready. There would be no test flights—no time for it, sadly—and so, with a sweaty hand I waved to the people outside our craft.

One mean heaved, and our mooring lines loosened. The exit from this structure was the first challenge, one of the most dangerous parts of this whole endeavor. We floated, almost at the same buoyancy as air, and could easily hit the sides or the roof if we weren't properly careful.

Slowly, so very slowly, we inched forward, watchers making fine adjustments and Chien and I sat in the cockpit, jaws clenched.

And then we were free. The lines were released and we began to rise, a slow, controlled thing. Below us there was a cheer from everyone who'd gathered, everyone who had come to see my next invention, who worried about monsters that were still so far away but seemed so close in everyone's minds.

Isha and Adia weren't there, though. They were back at home. That had been my call, for there were only two ways this could go—extremely well or extremely bad. I was pretty sure this would go well, but if it didn't, I didn't want my daughter having nightmares. No, today they'd only see us as we passed by the compound, floating overhead.

As we did so, I saw a flash of sparks down below—a signal we'd agreed on ahead of time—and I sent my own, as well, a farewell to my family. The home I'd built seemed so small from up here, almost like a dollhouse. Goodbyes said, we lurched upward.

The city shrank, falling back from us as we shot toward the clouds. I could see the walls, the fields, the homes, and everything from up here. I'd never gone this high with my own magic, afraid of falling, but now it seemed much safer.

"I'm glad the crystals work," Chien said with a smile.

"That, at least, was never in doubt."

I did not yet have the tech to kludge together a proper propulsion system for a blimp, so I'd taken shortcuts. Sure, my computers didn't work yet, but I could still make crystals of kinetic energy that just pushed in one direction. A bundle of these aimed in various ways was our system of movement, and while it was crude, it worked. Much like the heating stone that kept Icehome warm, this monstrosity would take us where we needed to go.

The land moved below us at a good clip, faster than going on foot, lower than a bird, but consistent. It would still take days, but if Chien and I traded off, we could get there pretty quickly.

There were, of course, other problems, like visibility and wind. Without GPS or any sort of ground aid, we had to rely primarily on looking down and guessing. Someone from my previous world might have been able to come up with some form of navigation based on the stars, but that wasn't me; I'd briefly tried. No, instead we'd be going on a really basic reckoning with a compass.

My craft was . . . Well, honestly, it was a bit janky. It pulled to the left slightly, shook something fierce whenever we accelerated—all the hallmarks of a car about to die, but it flew, and that was magnificent.

"Well, boss, we have snacks, a beautiful view, and a long time to enjoy it. Maybe we should sing or something to pass the time."

"Good old-fashioned road trip," I mused.

"There aren't any roads up here."

"Yeah, perhaps not, but air trip doesn't sound the same, does it?"

"No, suppose not. How long do you think this will take?" We'd barely left view of the city at this point.

"Less than a week? Depends on how we do it. Little worried about flying through the night, though; visibility will be a beast." And after a bit of thinking, I added one more condition. "And, if you start asking me if we're there yet, I will throw you out of this balloon."

"I can fly, boss. You know that. Not well, granted, and I puke every time I do it, but I can still fly. And why would I ask you? Don't you remember the tree? We'll see it long before we get there, and it will be painfully obvious when we get closer."

"Just a thought," I said with a smile.

"You're weird sometimes, you know that?"

"Suppose I am, but would you have it any other way?"

"Not a chance, boss. Without you, my life would be boring, and honestly I'd be pathetic, in all likelihood."

"That's not true, Chien. I remember when we first met. You were a right little rascal, and always trying for more."

"Well, I was a bit of a scamp, wasn't I? Sometimes I miss those days."

"Everyone feels that way about their childhood, but honestly, it would never be like we remember it if we could go back." I spoke from experience. While I'd loved both of my youths, it wasn't like the second one was much like the first, and the creases showed more during that time. I saw the failures of adults, the pain I'd missed the first time around.

"Yeah, guess not. Still, though."

We spent hours chatting until night began to set in. We really couldn't do much but try to keep high enough and going straight.

Most of our journey was uneventful, just two old friends eating snacks and talking about old times. Chien did manage to get me to join him for some singing at one point, revealing to me songs I'd never heard from him. Neither of us could hold a tune worth a damn, but that didn't matter; it was all good fun.

We looked on in horror when we passed over the pines again. The first time we'd come we'd seen the beginning of pollen season, the explosion of color from the trees that we'd run to avoid. Now we saw it once more from above. Below us the ground looked like a roiling yellow sea—trees like rocks in shallows poking up here and there beneath the cloud of yellow. I didn't see the waterfall we'd come up last time. We'd probably missed it by many miles, but that changed little, and onward we went.

Three days in, the trees began to grow in size, reaching up toward us. There were probably villages down there somewhere, looking up in horror at what must have appeared to be a massive monster flying past them.

On the afternoon of the fourth day we saw it. Above the rest of the trees one reached toward the heavens like an outstretched hand. It was no different from the last time I'd seen it.

"Is it bigger?" Chien asked.

"No, just a better view. Get ready. We'll arrive around sunset, assuming we're not met in the air by curious observers."

CHAPTER 24

RETURN TO ROLAN'S

We did not make it to Rolan's tree before we were intercepted in a major way. A flying wing of elves rose from the canopy, heading straight toward us, looking none too pleased as we closed in on the city. Well, a wing might have been an exaggeration. There were only eight, and they were hardly in any kind of formation I could identify. At least our guests didn't attack before getting closer to investigate.

On Earth, we'd have had to radio down, use call-signs, get permissions on where and when to land, and all that nonsense that pilots had to deal with. This world, however, was a bit different, and rather than go through any of that, Chien just leaned out the window and waved them to us. A few moments later, an elder crawled through that same window, looking extremely unhappy.

"Who are you, and why have you brought this beast to our home!" he roared.

"What beast?" I asked. "Oh, and I'm Justin. I was asked to come by Rolan and the others."

"Wh-what beast? The beast you've strapped this box to, you fool!"

"This isn't a beast; it's basically bags of air."

"How in the name of the forest is that supposed to work?!" He seemed to not believe me, and was quite unhappy.

"That's a long explanation which, if needed, I will give to Rolan. Now, where should I land?"

"Remain aloft for now," the elder replied. "I will consult the ancient on where he desires this . . . thing."

As he jumped off the craft and back into the air, I heard the laughter behind me, my assistant barely able to breathe.

"Don't laugh yet. If they decide to take us down, we'll be in for a world of trouble," I told him.

It was true, too. This thing had too much ordinance to do anything but go down in a ball of flames and poison. Whatever was below us would be thoroughly cooked, and I couldn't risk it all falling into the hands of a potential enemy. If it came to it, I'd destroy the whole thing rather than let it be captured.

"Don't worry," Chien said with a smile. "Rolan is good people."

"I know, but that doesn't mean everyone below him is, and no small few could cause real trouble."

It seemed there was little to worry about, though, as soon the large tree we were heading toward began to shift slightly. In the end, it was only branches moving by a few degrees each, but when dealing with a plant bigger than skyscrapers, a few degrees wasn't a small thing. It was followed by a flash pattern inside the hole the moving branches had made, one I recognized as the signal for "safe" from long ago.

"All right, slow and steady. Let's bring her in."

"Her?"

"All ships are female," I replied. "Didn't you know that?"

"How is this a boat?"

"A sky boat."

"We were calling it a blimp though?"

"Is it really the time for this?"

"Why not?"

With a sigh, I just shook my head and got back to the job at hand. There was clearly a landing spot for us, and while steering was . . . poor, that didn't mean we couldn't slowly bring it in. If nothing else, I could just adjust our trajectory and speed with my own magic. It was tiresome, but easy enough.

Surprises continued, though, as there was a crowd on the branch we came into. Rolan was there, casually causing vines to carefully move to our mooring points and yielding a cradle to grow beneath us, all the while looking a bit surprised. There were dozens of elders, most clearly much older than myself, including Jina.

"So, they called you out here, too?" I asked as I landed, having not been informed.

"Indeed," she confirmed.

"We needed everyone we could get," Rolan added. "Most of the elders of Atal are poorly suited for what we're doing—too young or too specialized for other things—but you two will be a great help."

"And what are we doing exactly?" I asked.

"Going to kill those beasts. I hope you brought enough . . . whatever it is you do," Jina explained.

"On another note, did you threaten my messenger?" Rolan asked. "Why?"

"Because he's an ass and didn't give me any details. You really should have provided more details."

"To be fair," Jina added, "I wanted to beat the man, too."

"Let's put that aside. Did you bring weapons?" the ancient inquired.

"Not as many as I'd have liked, if we're to go to war, but a few. Get me where I need to be safely, and I should be able to contribute well."

"We can arrange that."

The two gestured me to follow, and we made our way toward the tree proper. With a look back I could see Chien lounging in the cabin of my blimp, giving me a thumbs up. He didn't need to be there for what came next, and probably didn't want to. We needed someone to watch the craft, anyway, so his choice was what mine would have been. He could and would make sure nobody messed with things.

There was only one more surprise before the meeting.

"What is that abomination?" I asked, looking at the tangle of ropes around the hanging platform.

"Ah, the new elevator. My own inventor changed it to go along with your suggestions." Rolan seemed almost proud for some insane reason.

"He clearly wasn't paying attention."

"Come now, it's much better than it used to be."

"I'm flying."

CHAPTER 25

MEETING OF ELDERS

I wasn't given a moment to rest, nor much time to chat with my new companions. Instead, we were led to a massive chamber. Everywhere I looked there were elders, some clearly from the north with their pale skin and light hair, some in the clothes of the swamps, some I knew from my own home in Atal. There were at least fifty, most in small groups and deep discussion.

And, some were . . . flirting. That surprised me, but then I remembered who we were. Many of our kind came to dislike each other over the years, and with how long we lived, marriages fell apart sometimes. Isha and I had pretty much always been together, but these people? Many had had many lovers, and the sheer breadth of potential mates for powerful children in one room was nothing to scoff at.

It was a known fact among my people that powerful parents made powerful children. It wasn't a sure thing, of course, and plenty of strong people came from those without a bloodline, but it was a very, very strong trend. I didn't know why—genetics, some form of magic in the seed, something like that. While magic seemed to follow physics, I'd seen enough of this world to guess there were cases where it didn't. Isha's magic, for example, seemed to mostly obey physical laws, but also cheated in ways I personally felt almost insulted by.

A few faces nodded to me in recognition, or smiled, but many of the people here blew me off. Among the many elders were others, aides clearly, or assistants they'd brought along. Perhaps these older elves thought I was an aide, and not someone here for the fight. That was fine. I'd show them when it came time to do what needed to be done.

"Elder Justin has arrived," our host announced as we came in. "He hails from Atal." He turned to me. "Most of us have arrived now, but we're waiting another five days for stragglers. I encourage you to mingle, try to see where you will fit in best, and what we'll all be bringing to the fight."

Taking his advice, I moved into the room. I avoided the more flirtatious elves, for I had no need of them at all. Instead, I moved toward a group with much more serious faces.

"If they're actually using fire, or spreading it, we'll have to deal with that. You can't use fire magic against a fire being, of course." An older man was leading the discussion, looking toward a pale woman as he spoke.

"Probably heat resistant," I chimed in, "but we can use fire in other ways."

"What ways?" he asked.

"Denying them food, or perhaps air. I don't know if these specific beasts need it, but smoke can kill."

"That's . . . not the worst idea I've heard today. I'm Olar, and you're Justin, yes?" he asked.

"Indeed." As he spoke I heard tones that reminded me of the forests nearby, slight changes in the way he said things that told me where he was likely from.

"I heard about you, but we never talked," the pale woman said. "Rumor is you really peeved the matriarch."

"I really peeve a lot of people," I pointed out.

"What do you do exactly?" Olar said. "If you're here at your age, you must be some kind of expert."

I blinked, taken aback by the slight respect I heard in his tone. Perhaps it had been the people I'd been dealing with. Perhaps it had been the constant fighting with all the local elders that I'd been dealing with. Honestly, it was extremely refreshing.

"My thing is building things, like the blimp that I came in."

"The what?" he asked.

"We just came in a few minutes ago, big roundish flying thing."

"Oh, I saw that!" the woman, whose name I'd still not learned, enthused. "Did you make it yourself? What kind of monster is it? Can you take others up there with you?"

"Yes, it's not. It's a machine, and not really; the place for people is very small." In retrospect my social skills might have stagnated, a lot. Probably should work on that at some point.

"A shame, but perhaps you could take me up there at some point?" she suggested.

"Perhaps." I turned back to the man who seemed far more serious than most. "Have we received any in-depth information on fighting these beasts yet? So far as I know, none of us have gone up against one yet."

"We killed one," one of the others in the group croaked out. "Lost dozens against it. They spit fire, are hard to hit, and faster than something that size looks like it would be. Also the meanest bastards I've ever come up against."

"Are they smart?" I asked.

"Smart?"

"Did they use traps, group tactics? Did they change tactics or focus on certain things above others? Or are they just brutes going after the first thing they can?"

He leaned back, eyes seeming unfocused as he went through his memories, undoubtedly playing back the whole incident in his mind. It happened sometimes when we reached for what we'd seen before.

"The one we went after was alone," he began after a while. "And we caught it in a trap rather than the other way around, but it wasn't stupid. It quickly realized that going against our strongest first wasn't working and went for the back line—supporters and healers were its first targets. I didn't realize that at the time, but thinking on it now, it avoided me and the other more powerful attackers, going for the weakest first."

That wasn't too surprising. If these creatures were taking over entire areas of our lands, they had to be at least a bit clever.

"Please, go into detail if you can."

As he began his tale, everyone leaned in to listen.

CHAPTER 26

DUSK

I learned a lot about our enemy, but sadly nowhere near as much as I might have liked. From the sounds of it, they were a lot like dinosaurs, and for a time I thought they might be the dragons whose bones I found in that cave, or some related species. But they lacked wings, or the right kinds of horns, if the few drawings people made were to be believed.

However, they still couldn't fly, and I could, so . . . air of superiority it was, I guess. This idea got a lot of traction but, though many of the people here could make their way into the air, not all could. Even those that could often found it disorienting and slightly difficult, so I was happy I wasn't alone on that one.

Things like that seemed strange to me, like that almost nobody tried to learn to fly. Sure, it was hard, but the advantages were so clear. Wait, no, they were clear to me. I had come from a place where flying had been exploited for nearly a century by the whole world. Here, only a few people had magic, and they didn't always share, and of those few, not all could even attempt the spells for flight. There was a hard cutoff, and not knowing meant nobody worked to innovate for it.

Paradigms were important, more important than technology. I'd been focusing on one, but the other was either just as or more vital to a growing society. Perhaps it was time to try and figure a way to get those worked into my home now . . . whatever that might be.

"You look contemplative," Chien said from his part of the cabin.

"Thinking about how to build better."

"So nothing new then?"

"Haha."

"Since you're back with me now, how many are here?" he asked.

"All of them, it seems." He just blinked at my words. "The whole council is here, or at least all the elders, as well as every single one I know of."

"Whoa, how did Rolan manage that one?"

"I suspect he made a lot of promises he knows he won't have to keep, as did the other old ones."

"He won't have to keep?"

"Not everyone is coming back from this, Chien. A lot of people aren't, if even half of what I've heard and what he expects are true."

"Boss, are you sure we want to be part of this?"

"No, but honestly, we can't back out at this point. If we did, we'd just be inviting someone to make an example of us. More than that, though, we're going to be safer than any of them, I think, and if needed, we'll flee."

He looked serious for once, and that was good. I wasn't sure what we were going for here, but I didn't really want to try bringing any more of my power to bear than I already had. It wasn't like I could fit much more into the blimp either way. What we had would have to be enough.

"If that happens, boss, make sure you get out." That comment made me turn and look at him.

"No, Chien, you're the one who needs to flee first."

"Wrong, as you too often are. If I die, nothing major changes; if you die, everything falls apart."

I frowned, not liking his words one bit. "Absolutely not, you're not expendable."

"How about this then?" he tried with a smile. "We stick together, and if we need to flee, we flee as one; if we need to fight, we fight alongside each other."

"You're not giving up on this, are you?"

"No."

"Uggghhhh." Isha was going to kill us if something went wrong, both of us, painfully, slowly. "Then we go back together."

"I'm glad you agree with me," he said. "Now let's try not to do anything too stupid and over the top."

"Whenever have you known me to do things that are stupid and over the top?" I said, trying and failing to keep a straight face.

"Are you two done yet?" came a voice from our door, an unhappy looking Jina standing there—well, more unhappy than usual. She'd shown herself right to our doorstep.

"No," we answered in unison.

"Well, put it away and come along, you," she said to me. "We need to discuss where we'll all be during this."

"I will be near the clouds, raining death upon our enemy," I said placidly, managing to actually keep my face straight this time.

"And you will still come to this meeting; now hurry."

She reminded me of some of my teachers from my first childhood, the ones I didn't like. Now, Jina still did some things I really liked, but she was almost always sour. While her manner mattered less to me than her actions, it still could use serious improvement.

With a sigh I rose and followed after. We headed toward a platform above us, newly grown. No longer could the meetings be held inside, for if we kept on like that, we might well jeopardize the integrity of the tree, so this flattened space had been added for us, a place where we could all meet.

At the front were Rolan and Neera, the two ancients, their pure white hair shining in the evening sun. The former was clearly the leader. At this point, I knew enough about what the latter did to realize she was probably far weaker than her companion, but we needed her all the same. I joined Jina and rank after rank of elders and soldiers, all with serious faces, all looking toward the two that would take us into battle. Below us, I could see dusk begin to take the forest floor, but we'd have a little while before it rose to us.

"We leave at sunrise," Rolan declared. "Here will be our groups."

CHAPTER 27

UNWELCOME RIDER

As the first rays of dawn lit up the canopy, our army came to life. Like ants moving in a swarm, I could see the land-based troops below making their way toward the roads. Nobody except us was flying yet, but I was sure when the fighting began, at least a few would see the benefit.

Ropes were thrown off and moorings loosed. We rose, taking to the air above our compatriots, well, most of them.

"You could have at least brought in another seat," complained Matriarch Neera from atop a pile of munitions.

"You were not planned for, nor invited to join us in here," I responded unhappily.

Most were not willing to speak to her like that, and it showed. She'd all but forced her way into our cabin, and the small woman was not taking up space we'd told quite a few people they weren't welcome to have.

"Walking that far would be exhausting, and I do not have the magics to undo such tiredness, nor do I wish to waste my energy flying."

"And so you're coming to bother us? I'm sure you could have found someone to soothe your muscles and feet, Matriarch, rather than insist on getting into my very small vehicle."

"It's not so small, and I'm light. You could have easily had four or five people in here with you."

"And if one of them mishandled one of the small pots in that box you're sitting on, we'd all die in a brilliant ball of fire." That wasn't specifically true, since they would need to be lit before being dropped, but it could happen.

The little ancient looked at her seat with a clear amount of worry. At least she didn't doubt that I could make potent weapons. Good, let her think about how terribly rude she was being. I also felt her begin weaving a shield around herself, going against what she'd claimed about wasting mana. Not that she didn't have enough to spare while we traveled.

Chien, of course, said nothing. While I might be able to mouth off to someone as old as her and get away with it, I suspected he believed he wouldn't get the same grace. Personally, I was a bit taken aback by that, since if she actually did anything to my assistant, I would personally have gone nuclear on her.

Neera began peppering me with questions about the craft.

"So what's in these boxes?"

"Various things, mostly nasty ones."

"That's hardly an answer."

"It's the best you're going to get," I told her coldly.

"Fair, but what about the craft itself?" she asked. "Why does it fly?"

"Why does a boat float?" I returned.

"Because it's made of things that float," she answered seamlessly and incorrectly.

"Why do they float?" I tried again.

"I don't know. Never thought about it all that much, honestly. Some things float, some things don't. How does it matter to how this flies?"

"They use the same principle."

"Stop speaking in riddles; it doesn't make you sound clever," she said from her perch, frowning deeply.

"Think about it, and then ask me again later."

That didn't improve her mood, but I didn't care, because it got her to shut up for a while. She did look to be thinking, though, going over what I'd asked in her head as we floated along. It wasn't like there was much for us to do, just some light steering and keeping an eye on the rest of the army below us.

As the sun got low, I saw the army of elders begin to make camp, a small circle of lights appearing down on the ground, and so we came down ourselves. We didn't land fully, but we'd get close enough to anchor to the ground and float nearby. Since all of us could fly, it wasn't an issue to pop down to the ground to cook or check in with the others.

While I was preparing our dinner, Neera meandered off for a bit, for what reason I neither knew nor cared. When she came back, though, she seemed keen to revisit our earlier conversation.

"It floats because it is its nature to float. Many things can, and do, but they do because that is their nature." Her explanation sounded like something from Greek philosophy.

"No."

"You sound so sure, so tell me if you think you've a better answer."

"Can metal float?" I asked.

"No, it's too heavy."

I took some spare parts I had on the ship—some nuts and bolts—and made a little metal boat.

"Go find some water and try it out," I instructed.

When she came back, she actually looked surprised, and sat beside me.

"How?"

"It weighs less than the water that would be where it is in the water." Trying to explain density without any preceding information didn't come naturally for me.

"So, because it is lighter than the water would be, the water moves down, like rocks in a lake." That was actually an excellent explanation.

"Yes."

"But your flying craft, what is it lighter than?" she asked, finally understanding.

"The air."

"When this is over, you should come work for me. You'll have everything you desire without any issue; I'll see to it myself. You can have women, foods of whatever kind you like, materials for your work, anything I can provide you." Her eyes were sharp, for even if she'd basically hidden away for most of her life, she wasn't a fool.

"I'm uninterested."

"You should reconsider. Others will see what you're doing and planning on doing. They might try to use force, but if you came to my side, none would dare to come for you or yours."

"If you're really that desperate to learn what I have to teach, all you have to do is come to Atal. I won't teach you everything, but I'm more than willing to teach you many things. For example, what I already have." As I spoke I nodded to the little boat in her hand. "Do try to be less of a pain, though."

Over the next few days she was considerably less of an irritant. She still insisted on riding with us, likely some ploy to get closer to us or learn what she could. Neera also asked questions here and there, nothing too deep, but things she was curious about, like the few dials and notes in the ship.

It was Chien who eventually broke down and gave her a basic rundown on my writing system, before working on putting as much math as he could into a lecture. He ran through a lot of the basics, even doing some light geometry over the course of days.

On the afternoon of the eighth day, though, he had to stop, for we had neared the mountains. Hills rose up as the peaks stretched toward the sky before us, and atop one of those peaks stood a creature that resembled a raptor from my days as a child playing with toy dinosaurs. All around it was nothing but fire, and it seemed far too big for what it appeared to be.

CHAPTER 28

FIRST BATTLE

No sooner had our target spotted the army than the thing charged. It raced down the mountain like an avalanche, causing one in its wake. Rather than snow, this was fire and stone—loose rocks kicked up mixed with blazing grass and dry plants—as it screamed and tried to dive into the arraying elves. From its mouth issued torrents of fire, mixed between balls that went far and a stream every time it breathed out.

Tried is an important word, for the elders had been prepping for this sort of aggression. Perhaps Neera hadn't been one of the main fighters last time these things came around, but she'd seen them before, and we'd received reports about this. Before the beast could plow into our force, shields were thrown up, layer by layer. The first couple were ineffective, resisted by some form of magic, but only the first couple. There was clearly some kind of limit to their resistance.

Once they reached that limit, though, all bets were off. The heavy hitters—Jina, Rolan, and Neera—all began to pour death upon the beast, with the southern leader, Uro, on the back line keeping things organized. The creature fell in seconds, roaring and screaming loud enough to shake the air before Chien and I could even get in the fight.

I couldn't hear the cheer go up from the crowd below, but I could see them moving, throwing up hands and jumping high in celebration of the first victory.

"Boss!" I heard from beside me as I looked down.

Three more of the monsters were starting to appear from the same hillock as the first. It didn't take more than a second for me to realize that the army couldn't see them, and instantly, I threw a hand out the window, sending forth a warning sign—brilliant lights flying in the direction of the enemy.

"We need to get over that hill, see if there are more," I told Chien as I began to steer us. "Prepare to shield us from any stray shots."

The blimp rose and we shot forward, pushing it to the limitations of its speed, which wasn't all that fast, but it was the best I had. As we did, the world fell back and away, revealing more and more of the landscape.

It took only seconds for me to see them—over a dozen more spots of fire burning in the surrounding hills. That was bad, but they weren't all converging just yet, merely going about their own business. Some were fighting other, smaller monsters, or feasting on kills; others were searching around them.

We were near a pass in the mountains, visible from where I was, and it was clearly charred black. That must be where they'd come through, and not too long ago, judging by the distribution and destruction evident.

However, that didn't remain the case. More screams of dying beasts rang out below as the army clashed with the three that had now attacked. The elders were holding, but it was plain to see that one creature had gotten very, very close to the front line, where it had no doubt been assaulted by spears and other weapons from the leading, physically inclined elves.

The dying screams of one monster had been enough to draw three, but the screams of those three seemed to change the metrics. Each and every blazing section below us sent out a streamer of fire, racing toward the fallen. Our enemy had seen that a challenger had arrived, and they were keen to put that foe to the test.

"Start with bombs; we need to delay them," I informed Chien. "If that many hit the army too close together, it's all over."

I was already sending out more warnings—flash patterns—showing there were many incoming, arcing toward the beasts as I tried to bring us between the army and where it looked like the largest concentration of flaming dinosaurs was.

Chien's aim wasn't great, his first few shots going wide, but his attacks were loud and left craters in the earth below. It caused the enemy some pause; that was something at least. With what I was seeing, I wasn't sure that those bombs would kill one with anything less than a direct hit, but they could slow one down if they hit nearby, make it stumble or fall, or just disorient one, for that matter.

Once I was happy with where we were, I got on the cannon and began to fire. My first shot went wildly wide, nowhere near where I needed it. The second, though, hit right in front of one of the dinos, sending up a spray of dirt that made the massive beast trip and fall. Before it could rise, a pale blue bolt from Matriarch Neera slammed into its side, making the thing thrash. It froze solid.

One after another we fought, trying to slow and delay them. That didn't mean we didn't kill any, though. Chien managed to score several direct hits, disabling or killing two himself. I managed only one, but the result was amazing. Cannonballs weren't magic, and while these things were tough, one to the face was enough to turn its skull into ever so many fragments.

The fight felt both incredibly quick, and as if it had gone on for hours. In truth, it had probably only been about one hour, from spotting the first enemy until the last fell, but that didn't make it any less intense. With a look out to check for more approaching and finding none, I handed control of the blimp to Chien and leapt from my craft to talk to the leadership below.

Rolan saw me slowing my fall and he, along with several others, came to meet me.

"That all of them?" he asked.

"All that I can see; how did we fare?"

"Ten dead, many more injured to one degree or another, and we need to rest."

"We might need to put that off for a few moments, if you're able," I told him.

"Why?"

"The pass they came through isn't far ahead. If we can block it, we can hold there and lick our wounds without worrying about more coming through."

"How big of a wall will we need?"

I gave him the rough dimensions, so far as I could tell. The pass was large enough—a small valley between two cliffs, probably carved by a river or creek over centuries or millennia, thousands of feet wide and very deep. With the elders and ancients we had, though, we should be able to manage something.

"Uro, you're in charge here for the moment. Matriarch Neera, Jina, Poran, Laba, Toar, and Shorin, please join me." He phrased it as a request, polite to egos, but it was clear he needed their cooperation on this now, not later.

I wove a platform for the healers, carrying us up to the balloon, while those with my same abilities flew in the direction I indicated. We'd fly in my craft, and while it would be standing room only, we had the room for now, since we'd burned through half of our bombs and no small number of the cannonballs I'd brought along.

"Glad you agree we need to close the gap," I said to Rolan as we sailed toward the hole the enemy had come through.

"None of those things can come through, or they'll cause more havoc."

"True."

As soon as we landed, Rolan got to work organizing the construction. The healers went first, growing trees to act as fenceposts and vines to connect and guide, while I and several others filled the gaps with rocks and rubble from the surrounding land. As each rock and section of earth was moved into place, roots and vines wrapped the construct tight, anchoring it in place. Rolan called out several times for more dirt than stone, or asked us to call water from the air to keep the plants alive, and quickly things took shape. The wall was ugly, but by dark it was fifty feet tall, ten feet thick, and stretched from one end of the opening to the other.

We'd won our first battle, and now it was time to lick our wounds and heal.

CHAPTER 29

CULLING

I don't know if anyone slept the first night at our newly constructed wall, but I know I didn't. I tossed and turned until I couldn't bear it anymore and just got up to keep watch. I was worried, deeply worried, that we might have another fight on our hands soon.

Fortunately, as the sun peeked over the horizon, there were no monsters, no beasts blazing across the fields to come and rip us to shreds.

"How are things?" I asked Rolan as I came to join him on the makeshift battlements.

"Poor," he replied, looking worried. "Some of the injured will need time to heal."

"I've seen you grow a wall in almost no time at all. Surely their injuries can't be worse than that? I know that most healers are limited, but they can't do what you can."

"Yes and no. I could repair the flesh on some of them—several of us could—but the long-term effects would be devastating. Even in just the next few days they would suffer greatly for it. This wall isn't made like the trees of my home; the plants within it will be dead soon. If we treated our best fighters the same, it would bode poorly for us."

"And here I thought you'd have found a way around it," I observed.

"While I appreciate the confidence, there are some things that are the way they must be." I wasn't entirely convinced that it was impossible, just that it was hard. That wasn't my area of expertise, though, so I'd defer to him on this, something he surely knew more about than I.

"How long do you think we'll need?" I asked.

"Three days, if I were to guess. That is assuming we don't run into any more of those creatures."

"I've seen none, but the time will be helpful anyway. We used much of our ammunition, and I'd like not to run out before all of this is done."

"You can make more in the field?"

"Yes; it will be lesser, but it can be done."

Early cannonballs had sometimes been made of stone, and that is what I would do. I wouldn't delude myself that they would be as good as iron cannonballs, but those had been able to kill pretty rapidly. We could hold the iron ones back, using them when needed, while instead pushing forward stone for general use. It could work, and would, at the very minimum, give us more shots.

"You did make quite the effect. Will you be able to do so every time?"

"Sadly, no," I informed him. "We used much of what we had because it had to happen, but if we run into too many groups of that size, we'll run out of everything quickly."

"Other options you can think of?"

"Not much that we can do here and now, I'm afraid. Though we might be able to put one or two more up there with us while fighting, if we know it's coming."

"If you're comfortable with it. Having one or two heavier hitters where they don't need to worry as much about defense will be a wonder for us. Though it might cause issues on the ground . . . We'll consult with the others before we leave."

While I made cannonballs, Chien rose up and scouted as best he could without going far. It wouldn't do for him to attract trouble or run into it without backup. While I worked, I thought. Most of what I was doing was pretty boring—just repetitive shaping of stone.

I presented my thoughts to the other elders and ancients, and as we prepared to leave, Neera joined us in the balloon. I got the feeling she liked it, and by the end of this, would probably want one for herself. Personally, I doubted she'd be able to put it to proper use, but if it got her to aid us, I'd happily make her one when this was all over, or just give her the prototype. That would be a small price to pay for sorting this out.

Our enemy, it seemed, traveled in rough groups. The size varied, but around a dozen seemed normal, from what Chien could see. Most of the time they just bee-lined for anything they thought they could reach, including other groups. My guess was that they were looking for other things to kill first, but these beasts were violent in the extreme, and if they couldn't find something, they'd settle for others of their own kind.

Slowly, our patrol approached a herd, aiming for one of the outliers. Above, we kept to our lookout, using the same light codes we'd always used to communicate. It seemed the dinos had no reaction to those, at least. That was part of my working theory.

"You're sure you can do it?" I asked Neera. "We're too far away for me to have any effect."

"Pfft, child, it will be no issue at all," she quipped.

The ground troops closed in, and as they did, her hands whipped out. There was no bright light, no explosion, no sign of anything serious other than a small distortion in the air. Her look of concentration, though, told me it was working.

My other hint that she'd succeeded was when the beast threw back its head and roared, or at least tried to. No sound echoed across the landscape, no loud call. That was my theory—that they communicated like that, calling for help or to alert others of their kind. Our main problem had been that we'd had to fight so many so unprepared, but now we *were* prepared, and we were the hunters.

"Are they moving?" I asked Chien from where he stood near me.

"No, no, no, doesn't look like any of them have sensed the attack."

"Good, then silence the cannon and start bombarding. No use letting this go to waste."

Our first target fell quickly, the group on the ground now familiar with how these things attacked, and striking hard and fast. Then the next, and the one after that. We couldn't clear the whole herd, unfortunately, as some stuck near the middle, close enough to each other to see one another. That was fine, though; we could come back. Better than coming back, it seemed probable that the remnant of this herd would meet another soon, and with their smaller numbers, they'd surely fall. More important was that we didn't lose anyone this time; there were some injuries, as to be expected, but no deaths.

One at a time, carefully, slowly, methodically, that would be our method. We would cull them, until they culled themselves to the point where we could end this. I also promised myself this—that when it was all over, I'd be making sure all the volcanoes were checked periodically. My guess was that these things had emerged from the eggs I'd seen, and I saw no reason to allow them another chance to raze our lands in a few thousand years.

CHAPTER 30

TRANSFORMATIONS

I awoke with a start.

"We've got incoming," Chien informed me.

Over the last week we'd gotten our hunting of the fire dinos down to an art, and I still needed a better name than *dinos*. There were still injuries, of course, and more than one loss, but we were making progress.

"How many?" I asked, rubbing my eyes.

"Five, not heading directly toward us, but to the southeast."

"There was another group that way, wasn't there?" I inquired.

"Yes, one of the larger ones," Matriarch Neera chimed in. "Last night we saw another small group heading that way, too, though nobody wants to try hunting these in the darkness."

"Odd, maybe we should scout it . . ."

The groups of dinos were moving constantly, a churn of violence that meant they rotated in and out every day or so. From what I could tell, they were just killing one another or moving elsewhere, often a mix of both. There was one thing, though. I never saw a group form, only fall apart. Perhaps that was because they weren't growing in number, or perhaps we just didn't have enough data points. I didn't know.

After a brief consultation, we decided it would be best to know what was going on, and began to sail in that direction. It didn't take too long before we got our first results. Though the location was perhaps fifty miles from our current camp, it was visible much further out.

A warm glow began, first over the horizon, like the dawn or the start of a forest fire, but as we got closer and closer, we began to hear them. The beasts were fighting something, and roaring constantly, the sound of it growing into an almost continuous tumult, louder and louder until I had to throw up a shield around us to block the sound. We'd still not seen what was going on, though, so we drifted closer.

"They're . . . fighting?" Chien said.

"Yes . . ."

We'd seen these things killing each other before. In fact, it seemed to be a distinct part of their nature—that they were homicidal, fratricidal, and prone to going after anything that moved. A few had even made noises at our balloon, but none could reach us, so we were mostly ignored. Violent, but smart enough to realize we were too far away.

Below us now, though, was what looked like a seething mass. Each monster ripped and tore into those around it, the fire that seemed to follow them around joining into a blaze nearly a mile wide. It was magic, of course. All of it was magic. They bled the stuff into the world around them—that was the source of the fire. Every herd of these things for a hundred miles must have converged on this location.

"Something's happening," Neera said with furrowed brows.

There, on one side of the mass, most of the dinos were dead, and one stood atop the pile, cut to pieces, bleeding and glowing as the surrounding flames licked at it. As it reigned over its fellows, the fires seemed to almost whirlpool around it, pulling inward. The creature visibly grew, and as it did, the others fled from it, moving quickly to the other sections of the melee.

"We need to hit them now before they can power up!" I yelled, having flashbacks of anime I'd watched on Earth, where heroes and villains waited for the transformations to happen. We wouldn't be doing that. "Cannons on target! Matriarch, hit that with everything you can!"

Swinging the blimp around to bring our weapon into line wasn't as fast as I would've liked, but the ancient with us didn't need that. She began forming a spell that dwarfed her previous attacks, taking only moments to pull it into shape carefully.

A second later, Chien began to fire, three shots striking near the target, but not one hitting. His fourth shot would have, but it was one of the stone balls, and it looked to almost melt in the air as the creature turned to it and the fire nearby responded. It now looked at us like a threat, fury burning in the monster's eyes.

There was a sucking movement in the flames as Neera fired her attack, and the dino did something we hadn't seen before. It opened its mouth as if to roar, but rather than sound it shot forth a lance of fire. The two attacks met like cruise missiles colliding, causing a shockwave that sent our balloon tumbling.

Boxes of ammunition flew, barely missing heads, cannonballs rolled, and I had to send out steamers of force to quickly grab what I could before it broke or fell away. The monsters fared worse. The collision having been near them and Neera's spell being stronger meant that much of the power went roughly downward. I could see pulped and broken creatures writhing where they'd been battling moments before. Even our attacker had been blown back, its jaw now hanging at an odd angle with bone protruding.

"Tell me you've got more of those, please!" I begged the matriarch, who looked a bit dazed as we spun to a stop.

"Not many," she admitted. "But I'll do what I can."

"Chien, toss the poisons, all of them. Another strike like that and they might leak. If you can hit their groups, good, but if you can't, just do your best. I'll shield while we retreat." I set us a new heading, knowing that if Neera only had a few, we might be in deep shit and began weaving together the strongest shielding spells I could think of.

For their part, our massed enemies didn't seem to care too much about the fact that we'd just attacked them, instead falling upon the injured. As they did, though, I could see more eddies forming in the sea of flames—five or six at least, in places where these creatures were entering the next stage of their life cycle.

Our fighting retreat was just that, a retreat. We didn't win, we didn't show great power. Sure, we killed a few of the creatures, the smaller ones, but I wasn't sure that would help at all. The survivors were getting bigger, stronger, and now had long-ranged attacks. Had our work so far in culling what we could, done anything at all? Had we managed to do any real damage? I didn't know, but it was clear that soon things would come to a head.

Neera, who was supposed to be a leader—one of our strongest—shook as we made it out of their range. She no longer looked like the fearless ruler of so many of our kind, but more like a scared girl, terrified of what was to come. Of course, she'd seen it before and was now reliving it again—the fury that would come for us.

CHAPTER 31

ROCKS FALL, EVERYTHING DIES

It was fortunate that the dinos had stopped attacking us before we made it back to our temporary base. The wall we'd built had worked as a staging point thus far, being made thicker and stronger, with a few support buildings here and there as we needed them. It was still pretty basic but would be a fortress before long.

When Neera and I landed near Rolan's command center, people saw us and realized that things were bad, us all but shouting that our attack hadn't gone to plan. Even the man himself frowned as we approached, silencing the other advisors around him.

"What is it?" Rolan asked.

"They're going through some kind of change, getting bigger, stronger," I told him.

"We can barely handle the groups of them we have now. How are we supposed to deal with that?" one of his people said.

"The good news is that they're killing most of their own, so there won't be as many, at least."

"Neera, your thoughts?" Rolan asked her. Up until now, she'd been silent.

"They're not at the level of the ones who killed the ancients, but they're getting there. If we don't act . . ."

"What have we already been doing if not acting?" Rolan asked calmly.

"I don't doubt it would be worse if we hadn't done anything, but we need to take this group out quickly, and move from here," I said, trying to calm things down.

"Any ideas, my fair inventor?" Neera sneered.

"Several, but most won't work in the time we have. One might, though."

With the numbers we had to deal with, who knew what we were going to be handling. I also didn't exactly have a chance to master some form of ice magic, something which might have been a better use of my time than building an airship, but hindsight and all that.

"Please explain, then," Rolan led.

"All right, here's how we start . . ."

It was a well-known fact that the defender had the advantage, and this world was no different. In any fight, those who could make the enemy come to them, who could arrange the terrain, the placement of forces, they had something the enemy didn't.

For this reason I'd let Chien take control of the blimp, for I felt I would be of more use on the battlements. There were only so many casters here, and they only trusted me so much, so this much was necessary.

He was coming back now, speeding along as fast as he could

while keeping shields focused below the craft. Ball after ball of flame shot toward him like fireworks at a celebration, following the craft as he brought it toward us. A few had gone along with him—elders who claimed they had fairly strong shields, ones who would be better there than here. After all, we had a wall.

"You sure this will work?" Rolan asked from beside me.

"No," I said with a shrug, "but it's the best I've got on short notice."

The first of the monsters crested the horizon, and we began to fire upon it. These things were dangerous enough, and there were elders that could easily hit things at that range, so there was no reason not to do it. Any damage we could inflict now would help later. It also ticked them off, which was useful.

Our opponents, no less than ten of them, finally seeing something they thought they could easily reach, began ignoring the blimp and charged us. I had to admit, for something that size, I did not expect them to be so fast. Each had grown, now around the size of a medium-sized building, and were barreling toward us. Bigger than we'd expected.

More and more spells began to pelt the creatures in waves. As one slowed, everyone moved to the next, trying to get them together, all in one spot, one centralized location. It wasn't easy, but we managed, just pulling the roaring herd into a pack, perfect for the next stage.

"This is madness," Neera complained from nearby as she threw wave after wave of projectiles. "If they make it to us, we'll lose so many! Your weapon isn't even magical!"

"They won't. Just bunch them up!"

As I spoke, the next part of the plan went into action. The beasts took another step, and the ground gave out. There were no poorly covered traps; we had better methods. Roots had gone under, and we'd dug out the bottom—huge pits—just the place to hold them. At the bottom of each were angled rods of stone, another attempt to just hold them.

The creatures fell a good twenty feet onto the stakes; though, from what I could see the damage was incidental. Those stones might have been enough against the lesser ones, a simple trap to kill one or two, but these were a bit tougher, the points of stone barely piercing their hide. It did keep them busy, though.

"NOW!" I shouted pointlessly, tossing up a flare.

The people above us, on the sides of the mountains surrounding this valley, didn't need to be told. I'd brought all these explosives, but against fire monsters they were . . . not as useful as I'd hoped they could be. However, when holes were drilled into rock faces and the bombs carefully lowered in . . . if I'd done the math right . . .

There was a crack, and a cliff face sheared off from its moorings, seeming to hang in the air for a moment. Slowly, ponderously, it began to move, down, down and away from the rocks it had once been part of. Who knew how much stone there actually was, but it had to be thousands of cubic feet, at least.

With a thunderous crash it fell upon our trap. My aim had been a bit off, but a bit off was still close enough to drop a fair chunk of mountain onto the static targets. They screamed like terrified and injured animals as boulder after boulder slammed into them.

It wasn't perfect—a few of the reptilian creatures struggled and tried to crawl from the wreckage, pulling themselves upward through the rocks and debris—but it was enough. With them injured, broken, and still we rained death upon them until nothing moved, and then for a while afterward, just for good measure.

"Well that worked," Rolan said, sounding almost surprised.

"Good, let's see if we can do it again."

CHAPTER 32

MISSING ENEMY

Trying to do it again was a bit of a failure, mostly because of where we found ourselves today.

"Nothing again, I'm beginning to suspect we may have a problem," Uro, the leader of one of our scout groups, said.

"They're not gone," Neera seethed. "And not going to go on their own, just ran off somewhere."

"We agree on that much, at least," I added. "From above it looks like the worst of the destruction is toward the northwest."

That was only a really general truth. I'd managed to find several places that looked like they'd been subject to the whole slaughter evolution thing we'd seen ourselves, but from there? The paths of fire headed away from us. In some ways that was very reassuring. These creatures were no longer headed toward our homes and people, but that also meant they were going somewhere else, for some other purpose.

Over a week had passed since our fight against the evolved dinos, and in that time we'd found only one more small group. A herd of three of them, all beaten and broken nearly to death were upon the ground, near one of the sites. They'd succeeded in taking the next step, but only after nearly killing themselves, making them an easy mark.

"So why are they leaving?" Rolan asked.

"Animals return home to breed," I said, grumbling a bit. "What if these are doing the same?"

I couldn't tell them about salmon from Earth, but the image flashed in my mind now. They struck out from their youthful home, heading toward the ocean to grow. And grow they did, into much more powerful, much stronger versions of themselves. Only then did they return home, losing many of their number along the way, breeding the next, stronger generation. Were these monsters like that? Did they migrate only to return home with the best of their kind?

"If they're leaving, they may be done. Many creatures that go home to breed die there," Rolan contemplated. "We've several species of bird like that, but there's no guarantee, is there?" he mused.

"No, and if they survive and are stronger . . ." I let the statement drop.

In my mind, I saw the eggs I'd seen so long ago, piles of them by the oddly resilient skeleton. These things didn't die easily, and their bodies stuck around. Some of them had even had parts harvested—skin and bones for weapons and armor. A few of the elders thought that the organs might be used in some unguent or another, though nobody had worked with them before.

Matriarch Neera had even taken a few things, and I looked at them now. Several mana stones now hung around her neck.

"Looking at them again?" she asked. "If you wanted them, all you needed to do was say so."

"Could you use them like you did the others?" Uro asked, looking at me.

"Others?" Neera inquired.

"No," I responded without elaboration.

"Now, hold on. What did you do with stones like these before?" Matriarch Neera asked, others looking on curiously.

"Killed Uro's counterpart. She'd threatened my people, and I took exception."

It was easy to forget that—compared to all the people I was with on this expedition—excluding Chien—I was still a youngling. They treated me with respect, with caution sometimes, but still listened to what I had to say. With the other elders, it wasn't so, but with me, they heard what I told them and heeded my advice.

And now these people looked at me with a mix of interest, and slight worry. For I'd revealed something they may have suspected but now worried about. I could use the power of mana stones, though they didn't know that it was only with the ones I made. If I let that secret slip, there could be real problems, like one of them figuring out how to do the same.

"That's unfortunate to hear," Neera said, removing her own and putting them away, probably just in case. "We might have had more weapons we sorely need."

I huffed; she wasn't wrong. If I'd had time to prepare—plenty of it, rather—then we might have had something more effective. The sad fact was that I hadn't had years or any experience with these things to know what would work.

"A shame. So, do we go after them and into what is definitely their territory?" I asked.

They all nodded agreement, for we all knew there was little else to do. We had to kill these things, or we could doom our whole civilization. Personally, I wanted to make sure those eggs were well and gone, too. Why would I leave something like that behind for myself or my descendants to deal with, after all? Had I known what would come of them, I might have sought to destroy them years ago. Not sure how I would have gone about that, as weak as I was back then, but I could have figured something out.

Weapons weren't the only thing, though. We'd already proven that. While I may not have ice cannons, or some massive freezing array that could lay low these beasts, I did have one or two ideas. There were other things in this world, like the mountain we'd used, but so, so different. We just needed to bring them to bear if it became necessary, if all else failed. If our war-band proved not sufficient enough, there were still a few things we could hope for that might manage to save us.

With those thoughts and a small smile, the barest bits of a last-ditch plan was formed. It would take some doing, some time, and some risk, but just perhaps . . .

CHAPTER 33

FAMILIAR FACE

Our lack of enemies continued, so we slowly made our way westward. The blimp could easily outpace the war-band but that would defeat the point. That was one thing losing most of my ammo had given me at least—we were much, much lighter. At least when nobody was riding with us.

"I can see why Neera likes this so much—much easier than walking," Uro said.

"I really need to start putting my foot down with you lot joining us up here," I grumbled.

"Relax, I'm not planning to overstay my welcome by too much. I just wanted to talk to you two for a bit and would prefer to do it privately."

"Not wanting the others to hear what you have to say?" Chien asked. "Naughty."

"More than that, I want to make sure you see what we're dealing with down there. See, you two are almost always apart from us, always above, away. It wouldn't be surprising if you weren't really aware of what everyone is thinking."

"And what are they thinking?" I asked.

"There's much grumbling; people are mad that we're seeing nothing at all now."

"You think they'd be happier that they're not in life or death battles," Chien quipped.

"You would, but they're also starting to act like this might be a fool's errand. Like the beasts are gone and we can go back to how things were, regardless of what was said before. If we don't find some soon, they may try to split from the expedition."

"Depending on how many go, that may leave us severely weakened."

"We're already weakened," Uro pointed out. "We should've had three more ancients and several more aged elders before this trip began. No, it will leave us nonviable if we lose too many."

"So, what do you want me to do?" I asked. "I can't exactly make them appear out of nowhere."

"This vessel is faster," Uro said. "You could scout ahead."

"And be cooked if we're not careful enough to get away from them. Regardless, I'm not sure that will be needed."

"Oh?"

"Yes, look."

I pointed out the front window, toward the far horizon. It was hard to see, but peaks were there. They were just a small, jagged line from where we were now, but I knew well enough that this didn't mean much. A day, two days, and we'd be at the western mountain range, where these things had come from, and where they were surely going. After all, that was where the volcanoes were, the ones where I'd seen their nest. Like salmon they returned to their spawning grounds, ready to make the next generation.

"We may need to see if we can find the volcano they went to before. I'm not sure if we're headed to it or not, but the trails on the ground look to be heading in the same general direction we are."

That was good enough for Uro to give his support, and though he said little about it, I could tell he seemed pleased we were closing in. There was nowhere for them to go once we caught up, nowhere for them to flee.

I took the night shift in the balloon alone, eyes scanning the horizon. Hours passed with nothing nearby—no animals, hardly any plants, save small shoots trying to worm their way out of the ground. So, I let my eyes range further and further afield.

Far out, and at the very edge of my vision, I saw what looked like a twinkling of light, a spot on the nearly blank canvas of the ground, mixed in with the few lines of black that showed where our enemy had retreated. I squinted but couldn't see it well enough—so small, so far—my eyes no match for the distance.

No matter, there were easy solutions to such things. I spun the magic from my hands and began to shape it, carefully, slowly making lenses and mirrors with nothing but my own power. I'd used similar instruments in the past, but with years to think on it, to reflect, to consider, I had made improvements.

The magical telescope projected out like a screen, the image hanging in the air as I brought the focus in, boosting power as needed. Fuzzy at first, but slowly resolving as pieces fell into place into what I was looking at.

It was white, purest white, and large. Two of the beasts were fighting in the far distance, too far for the noise to carry. Well, fighting might have been an exaggeration. One was slaughtering the other. The white one had another of its smaller kin by the throat and was ripping and tearing it apart, nearly taking the head fully off as I watched.

The look of it, the pure hatred it radiated, made me tingle, even from so far away. This beast—it was like the pale white egg I'd seen in their volcano so long ago. The memory flashed into my mind, and I wondered if this thing had hatched from that white egg, or maybe from another egg I'd not seen.

This had to be some form of mutant. It was so much larger than the other one, and looked even more vicious. Sure, it was hard to tell anything about size from this far out, but it gave off a feeling of danger.

As I stood there, contemplating waking up Chien, the creature's head turned, eyes locking onto mine. I froze. Could it see me? No, that was impossible. We were far too far away, even for a magical beast. The balloon, maybe. On the extreme end, that would be possible, as even if we didn't let off any light, moonlight would still play across its surface.

That didn't change the way it felt, though, like it was looking at me, just me, like it hated me. While the other monsters had radiated fury and violence, this one emanated pure, cold hate. This wasn't some beast that wanted to tear apart anything it found; this was a creature that wanted us dead and gone. It was almost human, almost like seeing the specter of death itself looking at me.

And then it turned away, huffing and striding off, after taking one last chance to tread upon its fallen enemy. I watched until the creature moved behind a hill, and I lost it, but it was clear it wasn't headed my way. That alone brought me some measure of peace, even as my skin still crawled.

I had gathered some information. It was male, obvious enough from the . . . member between its legs. I was pretty sure the one it'd killed was male, too, though we could check on that tomorrow, since it was in our direction of travel anyway.

Thinking back, most of the ones we'd seen tended to travel in groups of all one gender or the other, and that was odd, wasn't it? It hadn't much mattered to us so far, but there might be something more to it. I didn't know, and I don't suppose it mattered much, but it made me wonder why they did this, and if it had some deeper meaning we could use.

CHAPTER 34

TO THE FINAL BATTLE

Plains rose to form small hills, empty and burned to the ground, and rose quickly toward the volcanic mountains, the old beds from lava flows clear from high above. Well, at least it seemed like a short time from where we were. Perspective showed me things in real time as we moved, but the people on the ground undoubtedly had a different view of things.

Chien and I were separated from the rest of the group, and we grew apart from them more so by the day. It wasn't that we held ourselves above our fellows; more that since we spent little time on the ground, we didn't have the same view of things. They were seeing one angle, while we were seeing an entirely different one, and both were getting rather frustrated with the other.

Every time either of us went down to talk with Rolan, Neera, or anyone else, people made quips, complained about how we weren't getting there, about how nothing was being done.

The ground-based individuals mostly resented that the enemy seemed gone, and they were held together only by the ancients.

For our part, we weren't much better to them. They were so slow, and so frustratingly short-sighted. I could see the trails of destruction from above and track the beasts. Sure, it might not look like much from the ground, but from a sky-side view it was obvious where we needed to go. Our enemy wasn't exactly subtle, and I knew we had trackers among us who could've pointed the trails out, so why didn't they?

I had a feeling it was all going to come to a head sooner or later, and we needed to finish before that happened. If our party broke, we might not have the men to do what needed done, and who knew what the outcome would be. No, I wanted to speed ahead and find answers, but we needed to stay together.

It was almost too soon that we reached the base of the mountains proper, or at least that was what I thought as I looked back upon it later. Finding a way up and over was easy enough with me looking down from above, pointing to the gentlest slopes and nearest navigable valleys. Nobody with us knew this area well enough to be of help.

That wasn't surprising, since as far as I knew the villages beyond the range were gone. There'd been reports of a few survivors, but most of them, most of the people I'd met as we passed through? They were no more, burned to ash and soot by the monsters who now roamed the land. My memory hurt me here, as I could still see them in my mind, as if they were before me now, smiling and laughing, even though all were now gone or had fled as far as they could.

One good part of all this was that the sky was blessedly clear. There were no clouds, and the volcanoes that now rose up around us let off little in the way of smoke or ash. They were quiet, placid, waiting. Even the places where it was clear that rivers of lava flowed from time to time looked still and solid from up here. The reports from below confirmed it. None of these peaks had released anything in some time, perhaps since this disaster started.

More questions rose to my mind. Were these creatures somehow sucking the energy from the volcanic active region? Or was it the reverse—that while growing they fed into it, making what was normally a calm land into something wild and burning? Would our attack on them change things? Or did it even matter, since we had to do what we had to do?

A small blessing found us, and soon I saw it—painted at the very edge of my vision, a line of pale blue. Upon finding the ocean, I began to piece together memories, images, trying to pinpoint our place in the area. It was hard, trying to view things from the opposite side and above, but after consulting with Chien, we agreed. We were still a bit too far south from where we should be. The trails here were harder to follow than they had been, the ground long destroyed and covered in them from one end to the other. So we took our conclusion and began to steer the hunting party northward.

That night we saw it. We all saw it. It wasn't because the balloon was higher, or because I made some magical telescope, or anything like that. No, the reason was simple; the air glowed. It was all but impossible to tell how high the fires were, or how hot they burned, but they were burning. Every one of us saw the direction we were headed; all of us could see the light reflecting upward, scattering like light pollution of untold levels across the night sky.

The light got brighter and brighter, but never closer, peaking around midnight. After that it began to fade, slowly retreating into the horizon from whence it had come. I had a feeling, deep, deep in my bones, that we'd just seen the last of their little murder orgies. Whatever it was, it was done, and now we needed to end it, right now, before anything else could go wrong.

By Rolan's command we left at dawn, the army moving out in a tight and fast formation. Overhead I prepared every weapon I had, every trick I could pull out. This would be the moment, the day that we won or lost. No need to hold back anything either way.

"Are we ready, boss?" Chien asked, sounding nervous.

"As ready as we can be. Now, let me know when we can see them."

"The lava still isn't going, but they're here," he said after a short time, hands gripping the wheel.

Before us the volcano rose to the sky, the land around it cold and dead. Parts of it still glowed a bit, residual heat from what had happened the night before. The patches of hot rock were contained, though, small enough to easily avoid.

A brief look told me that the beasts had divided into two groups—one to one side of the volcano, the one to the other, then had gone about killing one another. While I couldn't be sure, my guess was male and female, all to leave only two of their kind, the two strongest. These two were near the peak now and . . . well, doing what animals did.

The female seemed no different to me than any other of her kind, though to survive this she must have been strong. Mounting her, though, was my old friend. It seemed the white dino had conquered all his fellows and was now claiming his prize. He would father the next generation, one that would harry our race again in another thousand years if we didn't do something about it.

I planned to do something about it.

CHAPTER 35

✧

BATTLE BEGINS

It was our spellcasters who started things off. Waves of cold and ice flew forward first, not just toward the enemy but also the ground, a path, a way for the more physically inclined to potentially reach the enemy. As they began, so did we from above, loading the last of the proper cannonballs and firing as fast as we could. There was no reason to hold back. This was the end.

"Chien, suspend yourself down as low as you can, safely. I'll shield; hit them hard!" I shouted at my copilot, who leaned outside with a nod.

He began to gather power around himself as I loaded the cannon again, moving as quickly as I could while still keeping an eye out for any incoming attacks. I'd seldom seen him cast aggressively. Normally, he let me handle it, but I wanted to switch between the two of us, and I knew I was still a bit stronger.

The coupling dinos had stopped, either finished or well aware that they didn't have time, and turned to face the rain of projectiles.

The female was projecting an aura outward, a technique I'd seen before myself, but not on so wide an area. She also struck out at the rain of cold and death.

Her counterpart had a different plan. He was charging up some kind of attack, slowly working it together like Chien was doing beside me, letting the female protect him as he formed the magic slowly around his mouth.

The magically empowered warriors, not wanting to be outmatched by their ranged counterparts, charged as one up the forming path, barreling like a wave of screaming death at the two beasts. They couldn't take them head-on alone, but if the creatures were weakened by the time they arrived, or distracted, they could still do some real damage.

Or they would have, had the male not released his attack then. A ball of fire rolled down the mountainside. It wasn't fast, but it didn't have to be. Around it the rock cracked, going from glowing red to flowing and molten as it rolled over the mountainside. The brave warriors who'd charged tried to dodge, but it was for naught. Heat cooked them. From above it looked like they just fell as it neared, some of them mid-run and crashing into the rock before being reduced to ash.

Neera's shield met it head on, causing the projectile to stop and shatter but burning away in the process. I could see her pale hair from up above, stumbling and nearly falling as her spell drained her and stopped the attack in the process. Others had taken up her cause, though, and though many of their shields popped like bubbles of spun glass, they held the line, preserving the main force. Uro was nearby, keeping her alive as well as he could with his own protections.

I'd have loved to keep attacking myself, but I had to begin preparing my own defenses, wrapping us in a thick, layered envelope, as that would be best to deal with the heat, focused mostly from below. If we were hit head-on, there would be no chance, but luckily, so far, we'd not been targeted.

Things happened fast, and before they'd even recovered, Rolan and Jina made their presences known. It looked like they'd been coordinating, and it was a one-two punch. Jina's spell cleared the way—a black bolt that absorbed the female's defenses as it flew over the long distance up the volcano. Behind it came a similar one from Rolan.

The ancient healer's spell landed true on the female dino's body, and a blackness crept over her torso. I'd expected death, but he'd either worried he couldn't do it in one shot, or instead failed to manifest fully. The female monster screamed in pain, agony, and rage. Stumbling, she clawed at her belly, the magic focusing there.

They'd targeted the eggs, her eggs. If his spell had worked, and I didn't doubt he had put his all into it, we'd won even if we lost. These monsters took themselves down to one mating pair, their strongest, and now their next generation was gone. Win or not, though, we now needed to get away from here, preferably after taking down these two. I didn't want either of these creatures coming to my home looking for revenge.

The female dino's screams intensified, as if she knew what had been done, reaching a keening pitch that made my ears ring, even from so far away. It was almost sad, had these things been worthy of any pity at all. That wasn't all, though; her eyes went wild and she turned, charging down the volcano's slope.

She'd been controlled, defensive, restrained, but that was gone now. Now she was a furious beast, intent on killing everything before her, aiming for the two who had caused her pain. The male was not far behind, roaring in rage as he made his way across the molten trail he had made. Both went right for the casters, who'd let their physical supporters charge forward, not that they'd be of any help at this point, except maybe to carry them away as fast as they could.

I looked up, realizing no attacks had come from us because we'd been distracted.

"Chien, what in the world are you . . ." I looked over to where he was and had my answer. "Oh shit."

A spear of force was blossoming from his hand, so charged that it glowed in the air, and it was still growing. If I'd tried to do such a thing, it would have taken almost all of my mana, but he was managing it. Taking himself down to a safe amount of mana probably wasn't what I was seeing; he was likely burning everything he had.

Preparing to yell at him to release it, I saw him reach into one of the pockets of his jacket and pull forth several glimmering crystals. Mana crystals. He'd made some. I didn't even know he could do that on his own, but he'd managed it, and they popped like sparks from a forge, streams of power flowing into his attack.

"CHIEN, LOOSE IT!" I screamed, feeling the power.

He obliged, and I had to grab him and hold tight as the backlash sent us tumbling. I yelled in alarm, he laughed like a madman, and below us I could see the spear land.

The only thing I could think that might have compared was a kinetic orbital strike. They'd been theorized back on Earth, and had been called "Rods from God," though I hated that name. A telephone-pole-sized piece of tungsten dropped from orbit and landed with the energy of a small nuke.

Our female dino hadn't been pierced, or cut, or crushed. She'd been rendered into mist. Where she'd been was now a crater, red cracks from whatever molten rock left over radiating out from where she had been a moment ago. It happened so fast I didn't even see the actual impact. No, the spear was just in his hand one moment, and she was gone the next. Even her male companion was thrown back, his white hide bouncing away from where she'd been. Shame he couldn't get both of them.

"Did I do good, boss?" I heard from my arm, my assistant looking like he could barely move.

"Yeah, let me take over for a bit, okay?" I'd chew him out later for going completely ham, but he looked like he was ready to pass out, and we might not get a later.

He laughed once, and I saw his eyes roll back in his head. He was out cold.

CHAPTER 36

✧

MATRIARCH NEERA

Matriarch Neera

The beast was nearly upon us, furious, but sharp like a blade, its eyes hard as ice and obsidian, teeth bared in anger. From my side I heard Uro shouting, and the young leader acquitted himself well, a roar of power escaping his lips and slamming into the beast hard enough to make it stop.

It wouldn't be enough, though, not for us to kill this thing. This one had gone the same way I'd seen the others do all those years ago; it was strong, potent, deadly, even to me. How long had it been since I'd seen something like this? How many years since my life had really been in danger? My, how I hated it.

I'd not wanted to come here, to join this mission. However, there were several things that forced my hand. One, I wanted the plains that had been vacated, and I had been readying to take them for some years now, getting all my people in order for the oncoming war. We'd even made some inroads, a few small outposts reaching out before this disaster struck.

The other reason was near to me—he and the other aged one throwing everything they could at this monster. Rolan had made it clear that if I didn't join and he survived, we'd have issues, major issues. I didn't want to be here, and he may not have lived had I not come, but if I didn't and he lived? He'd kill me and I knew it; we both knew it.

"Can you hold it?" he yelled at me over the din of a dozen of us blasting away with spells.

"Not for long!" I replied. Trying to keep my blasts from hitting our formation was struggle enough.

"On my mark! Three, two, one, NOW!"

If I'd thrown a stone from the front of our formation without magic, I might just have been able to strike the beast at this distance. Too close, but I obliged, forming a rope of force and cold and shooting it forward to wrap the creature's legs. It was close, too close, and as it stumbled, it landed upon the first rank, its massive head reducing a woman to pulp as it crashed down.

The oldest of us were at the back, but I could see the elders struggling even now from the heat alone. I would have loved to help them, but keeping my spell going was draining me fast. It was wrapping around the creature, though, digging into its flesh as the cold cracked and tore at its internal heat.

"Get back! It won't stay still long. Hit it if you can, but living is more important!" I called to my own people, hoping some of them would make it to tomorrow.

Our healers poured power upon the creature, but they didn't have time for the concentrated blast they'd sent against the other one. Others wouldn't have noticed, but I did. They were also flagging, running low on energy to continue casting. If we didn't win soon, we wouldn't; though, I still had a bit in reserve, enough to escape should I need to.

It wasn't enough. The creature's aura flared as magic hit it, dissolving like a snowflake caught on the tongue. With another roar it thrashed violently, snapping my snare and struggling to regain its feet.

A boom sounded from far off as it got up, a small black blur slamming into one of the monster's small arms and leaving it hanging by a thread of flesh. The boy above was proving his worth—that strike and the other enough to help more than any boy his age should be able to. When this was over, the next fight would be for him. Perhaps my companion wouldn't admit it, but whoever ended up controlling his knowledge would gain power far and above any other. The problem might only come from whoever failed to gain him. They might try to destroy him instead, something I was keen to prevent.

That was for later, though. The beast screeched in rage and let loose a blast of flames. Everyone who could shield themselves did, and those who couldn't, or were too far from one who could, burned. Uro died with little more than a cry of alarm. The healers had a few near them dedicated to protection, though, so both Rolan and Jina survived. A shame really.

"Another snare on my mark!" the other ancient called to me, but the monster before us rivaled our power, and it was not letting up.

The creature dove toward the group of healers, slamming its face against the pale shield. Its aura pushed against the magic of their protectors and shoved it aside like a landslide.

"Neera!" he screamed as the remaining good claw snapped forward, catching Jina and tossing her like a child's doll.

"No," I said, just loud enough to be heard. "Goodbye, Rolan."

There was a trick I'd devised long ago, one seldom used, save for the direst of emergencies, for the magic it drained was agonizing. I used it now. Above me hundreds of feet of space crunched together, the world itself struggling as my magic took hold of such a large amount of area and compressed it. With a final look at the betrayed ancient's face I made a small hole and flew through before uncompressing the region, leaving myself well above the battle, though heaving from the effort.

He'd forced me here, and he'd try to take the boy from me. That boy's magic was like mine, and he should be mine. With his help I might even be able to make that last spell work properly without draining too much, for there was certainly something I was missing that made it so difficult. No, I was done with him. We'd won, and now I could take my prizes and go. With the female dead, these creatures wouldn't come for me ever again.

As I rose, I saw the jaws snap down on the man's torso, sending a spray of boiling blood flying, along with his legs. All below the dying screamed, trying to just live in the inferno created by the monster's very presence.

That was no longer my concern, though, as I sped upward, fleeing this place. Let the creature have his prizes; they'd be his last. As for me, I'd go, up, up to the flying ship, up away from this. I could get the boy and his apprentice to sail us away from the death, away from the monster, and we'd live on happily after; I'd won.

As I ascended, though, so too did his craft, bobbing to the side and rising as fast as I'd ever seen it move. What in the world was he doing? Trying to escape me? I could punish him later; I was still faster. Then I felt the heat.

With shock, I looked down upon the oncoming fireball, smaller than the last one this thing had loosed, but still enough. It was ignoring the dying below so it could strike me and the flying ship. There was no time, no room, no chance of shielding strong enough to withstand it head-on. In a panic I tried to reach out and compress the world again, pushing forward as I worked to pull existence itself where I wanted it to be. My panicked aim was off, though, and the edge of my magic crossed with the fireball. One field of magic met another, and both broke apart violently.

"Oh," was all I had time to say.

CHAPTER 37

A MERRY CHASE

I'd seen both Neera and the fire approaching from below as I tried to get the hell away from this disaster. There was precious little I could do for those on the ground, like it or not, and dying wasn't on my to-do list. If I'd been closer, I could have perhaps thrown up a shield, or pulled a few people away, but I'd probably also have been cooked by that monster.

The creature had been fast, deadly fast, and went on a complete rampage after killing practically everything and everyone in the opening salvo. Magic or no, most of those people were just as fragile as any normal human behind their magic, and it was tearing through them like they were tissue paper.

Neera had run, a sensible choice, and done something below us that seemed to make the whole world *flex* for just a moment. The sensation from above was odd, as was the massive distortion it had briefly made. It felt wrong, strange, and bad for the environment, but I didn't have time to study it.

Shortly after taking flight, the monster had blasted another fireball at the fleeing ancient. She'd done . . . something in response. It felt like another flex, but one that didn't work completely. There was a huge shudder, a flickering, and streams of fire seemed to shoot in every direction, but I couldn't catch even half of the details.

One thing I could spare a moment for was weaving a small spell around Chien to keep him in place. This situation was already hairy, and I didn't want him getting hurt. A few kinetic straps with more flexible fields to hold him in tight would do a lot to avoid a concussion.

I took my airship high enough that the air started getting thinner than I'd like, noticeable to even me as I—not fought, not tried to rescue—ran. It was a good thing I did, too, for not long after, another fireball whizzed past us, hitting a nearby cloud and fizzling, continuing on. I wondered how high it would get, but honestly I didn't need to worry about that now.

A quick look below showed that our white-scaled enemy wasn't at all deterred by my flight, and seemed keen to continue the fight. It fired off several attacks, all missing because of the distance and my changing course. Perhaps they lost power at this range, but I still wanted to be nowhere near any of those.

It was some time until Chien finally stirred.

"Ugh . . . whoa, what are you doing!" he shouted as the whole ship tilted again.

"Dodging, glad to see you're up, sleeping beauty."

"Nobody thinks I'm beautiful, boss; handsome maybe, but beautiful? And what's that got to do with sleep? You say the weirdest things." I let the spell holding him in place go as he got up. "If you're still fighting, I was out for what, a few minutes? Feels like I was run over by a parade." He rubbed his eyes, clearly in pain.

"Almost a full day, my friend. The sun went down and came back up again. I was starting to worry. Hold on!" I had to turn the ship again, banking left to avoid another projectile. "Bastard's getting more accurate."

I saw him look out the window at the landscape below, our unwanted tag-along a small dot from this height.

"It's following us," he said, voice low.

"Yes, it is. We're going north, I've got a few ideas. Maybe we can lose it on the cliffs, and if that doesn't work . . . well maybe the cold will weaken it. This is clearly a creature of fire, and lizards don't do well in the cold." I left out a few more thoughts I had, things I really didn't want to do, but would if needed.

"Right, and there shouldn't be anyone in that direction for a while at least. Don't want that thing getting anywhere near a village. What happened to the others? They ran?" he asked.

I was silent for a moment, before shaking my head. "Some might have survived, but it was pretty brutal, Chien. If they did live, it's because that thing wants us. I think it understands you killed its mate. Don't suppose you can manage that again can you?"

"Those were all of my crystals boss, and I'm still not back to full after that attack."

"Shame."

"You can't?"

"Not without crystals of my own, and that thing's not exactly giving me a chance to rest. Don't worry, I've got a few plans."

“Don’t you always?” he smirked.

“Well, since you’re up, mind spotting for me? Dump everything we don’t need. Not much left, but if you think it can go, it can go. We’ll need food and blankets, though.”

He nodded and got to it. Even without using magic, he could do quite a lot, tossing bits and bobs out to lighten our load. We chatted as he did, trying to fill the silence with something that wasn’t terror or worry about the creature determined to take us down.

Both of us were of the same mind when it came to a few things. One was that while I’d love to kill this thing, getting away at this point would be just as good. A few weeks at home and we could build something that would do exactly that, even if it was just more mana crystals or a big screw-off cannon. Perhaps others would suffer, but my people would be safe, and that was more important to me.

Two was that this creature had a real vicious streak. It followed us for days on end, not taking breaks, not turning from its course. It wanted us bad. At least it wasn’t constantly shooting at us now, rather waiting between volleys until it got to a high spot along the ground. That didn’t mean it was falling behind, though.

Another two days passed before we came to the first thing I thought might impede the beast. Cliffs we’d come down that led to the glacial shelf rose up below us, a massive wall. We sailed straight over and onto the frozen wasteland, but the monster? No, it would have to climb, and with one arm that would be no easy task.

Twenty minutes after we soared over the natural barrier Chien called out.

"Turn left."

"Suppose our friend didn't fail then?" I asked as I did so, watching a fireball cut through the cold sky.

"No, looks like he made it to the top."

"Plan B it is then."

CHAPTER 38

ANGRY BIRDS

"This bastard is persistent, boss," Chien complained, not for the first time.

"Indeed he is; are we ready?" I asked.

"Ready as we can be. Think they'll bite?"

"If they don't, I don't know what we do. I was hoping the cold or injuries would at least slow it down, but we can't really head to Icehome if it's following us. I won't do them wrong like that."

"Pretty sure they'd do you wrong like that if they needed to, but I see your point."

Our unwanted hanger-on trudged along the sheets of ice behind us, and while I might not like him, I did have to admire his stick-to-it attitude. The creature seemed to not even need to sleep or eat, just going and going. At some point it would have to give out, worn down by the effort, but who knew how long that would take. At least the occurrence of fireballs had decreased.

Once my companion had been able to take the wheel, I'd slept, not quite as long as he had, but long enough that I almost felt bad about leaving him, almost. We were both tired, having not had a good chance to really rest properly for days, the chase wearing on, the stress from the battle, and the fact that we didn't have much food left. Water, at least, wasn't a problem; in a pinch, either of us could summon it from the air.

The sun rose, and though it was far, I could see what we were looking for. The crevice in the ice was massive, having taken us quite some time to pass the last time either of us had been up this way. I doubted the dino could jump it, or make a bridge, so it would serve to stop him. There were, of course, other complications, potentially for all of us.

We saw the first one right as we neared the crevice. A bird, one that looked as if it had been carved from ice itself, soared near our craft, seemingly very confused at what in the world we were. It didn't attack, though that could change. It just observed, coming closer and closer.

By the time we'd reached the middle of the large crack in the glacial shelf, a dozen or more had joined the first. Seeing that we weren't doing anything menacing, they got closer and closer. One eventually landed on a windowsill, and seeing that there was something clear and hard before it began to peck.

These things ate ice; that much I knew. They went after anything they thought might be ice, like my windows. That was no good for me, as I really wanted those, but I knew better than to attack or push it away. It might see that as an assault, leading to the whole flock deciding to do something about us.

I'd been thinking of potential solutions for a while now, so I tried one. I gently reached out with my magic and began to form a small icicle near the bird. It was pristine, shining in the light, better than my windows did.

The little ice bird turned, looking at the new addition happily, and accepted the gift for what it was, munching away at the bit of frozen water. Then it started trying to break into my cabin again. This led to me making more and more of the chunks, attracting increasing amounts of the birds, and repeating.

"Boss, there's a lot of them," Chien said worriedly. "How long can you keep that up?" Chien asked worriedly.

"Long enough," I told him with a smile.

Small alterations to where the ice was didn't seem to bother the birds, like making it a little off the edge of the ship. They cawed and snapped the little bits from the air, swallowing them down. That was good. What was better was when I started making trails, leading down and away, a trail of raining ice shards that our old friends seemed ecstatic to go after. They fell right to the far edge of the crevice, right into the path of our enemy.

The first few curious corvids made their way near the white-scaled monster, but other than making some noise, seemed content not to fight it, at least not until the beast decided it wanted to metaphorically throw hands. It snapped at the birds, and seeing us getting away threw a fireball in our direction. The dinosaur was obscenely angry by this point, and its attack blasted straight into the flock that was following along below us.

"Oh, you messed up there, friend," Chien said with a smile as he looked down.

“Indeed he did.”

I’d never actually seen anyone do something like smack a beehive with a baseball bat, but I couldn’t imagine the result would be too dissimilar. There were countless birds around and within the crack in the ice, and upon being so blatantly attacked, they all took serious offense.

A cloud rose from the crevice with a cawing scream, sending a rain of ice at the flaming monster. They circled like crows after a hawk, dodging and moving like a single organism, one intent on showing just whose house this was and who was really in charge here. I, of course, had no desire to dispute their dominance, and so we fled.

Unfortunately, they didn’t know that, and a few of them decided that our little balloon was a foe, as well, and began to bombard us. It wasn’t many, no more than a couple dozen, honestly, but there didn’t need to be many. Coordinated attacks slapped against our sides, not something we could dodge from far away, but fast, pursuing enemies launching rapid strikes.

By some instinct, or pure luck, they managed to start ripping into the coverings on the gas sacks themselves, releasing clouds from above us as hole after hole began to appear.

“We’re losing altitude!” I shouted as we lurched, slowly but surely feeling the pull of gravity bringing what had gone up right back down.

“Can we land?” Chien asked, scared.

“Hold on, we just need to slow ourselves enough to survive. Make it as far from here as we can and we’ll run for it once we’re down. I don’t fancy coming between that,” I nodded out one of the windows.

The birds were falling in waves, but as they did, others began to join the fray. Long ago I'd learned that these monsters had an odd reaction to fire. They didn't die, but those who were broken and injured had their pieces pulled together like some kind of magnet and into amalgams. A few of these were showing up now, small for the moment, but with each fallen avian, there were growing, cawing monsters ready to rip into any enemy they could find.

As the ground neared, I wondered what the odds were on either side. It couldn't be too good for anyone.

CHAPTER 39

FIRE AND ICE

As I watched the ground getting closer and closer, it was Chien who pulled me from my attempts to slow our descent.

"Boss, we should bail."

I wanted to smack myself. I was stupid, stuck in the thoughts of someone who couldn't fly.

"Grab the bedding, and we go!" I shouted as soon as I processed it properly. We'd seriously need those blankets.

The two of us leapt from the stuttering airship, icy wind screaming in our ears as we fell toward the earth like stones. I felt relieved, too, as our pursuer tossed an attack at it. We could perhaps have dodged before it struck, but now we would be well away.

Chien and I held onto one another as I threw up a shield and tried to arrest our fall. We'd seen just how strong those fireballs were by now. It passed hundreds of feet away, but I still wanted nothing to do with it.

I felt a pain deep within as the attack finally connected. After all that time dodging the monster's attempts to destroy our airship, it had finally worked, the flames rolling over the whole structure, reducing the cloth to ash and cinder and ripping apart the cabin like cotton candy in water. It ended with an explosion, further buffeting us as we continued to fall.

Chien took over slowing our descent as I tried to get a fix on what was happening. We figured it out without even speaking; no words were needed, as we'd been around each other so long we just knew. What I saw brought a smile to my face.

The white-scaled dino may have wrecked one of my favorite creations, but he wasn't enjoying himself at all. The birds were still harrying him, but more effective were the amalgam monsters. Around them was a cloud of shards, and though it was strong, quantity had a quality all its own, and the white flesh of the beast was streaked with red, and only getting worse.

As it roared in victory over the flying pest, it looked at us, though, and I saw recognition of what we were.

"Fuck." My words were ripped away by the wind, but Chien felt me stiffen and looked, having brought us down to just feet above the snow and ice.

Having found a new target, and quite frustrated with its avian irritants, the creature roared again, releasing a wide wave of fire. That was new, and quite unwelcome, as the flock seemed to fall, almost all of the birds and amalgams dropping to the melting ice. Then the creature turned and ran from the crevice.

"It's running?" Chien asked. We had made it to the other side, so we had a good view of the retreating beast.

"Why did you have to say it?" I asked as the beast turned around, bolting back toward us. This thing really might be as smart as a person.

The leap from the monster sent the whole section it had been battling the birds on tumbling into the darkness of the fissure, the remaining ice birds screeching and cawing as they fell. My heart lurched as the creature sailed through the air, legs extended and teeth bared.

Then it fell, missing the cliff by feet and slamming into the side as it disappeared below the edge.

"Is it gone?" Chien asked.

There was a roar as the beast's head flashed briefly over the edge, and a scraping of claws on ice.

"COULD YOU STOP SAYING THOSE THINGS!" I roared as I gathered mana for an attack.

As soon as I got a clear shot, I loosed a bolt at the monster's face, squarely hitting the eye and sending a fountain of blood out. It screamed again as it climbed, trying to make it up. Chien and I were hitting it as hard as we could, pummeling away at the weakened beast, doing everything we could to try and hurt the monster that seemed bound and determined to kill everything it could, starting with us.

The creature was weakened, with heavy injuries and days and days of running without rest. It was strong, stronger than us, but if there was a chance, it was now. This thing could take on ancients at its prime, but it was nowhere near that at this point. The cold and the monsters had done their job, injuries it had suffered helping to weaken the potent monster to this moment, when it was tired, spent, and still striving to go, but flagging fast. If we could just keep up the pressure a bit longer, I knew there was at least one last chance.

However, our enemy had ideas, too, and enough strength left for what it was doing. Even under our assault it clamored up, closing its remaining eye as it pulled its beaten body up the edge of the crevice, its one good arm grabbing at all it could to pull it forward.

We'd used so much of our mana, too, that as it rose and stood on the cliff's edge, I paled. Perhaps we could flee now, run, but I heard something that brought me hope. The sound of many wings, and cries of anguish and anger, mixed with the crackling of ice and incessant, interminable caws.

"CAWWWCAWCAHCAHCAWCAW!!"

Half the flock had to have been integrated into this creature that rose behind our shared opponent. It was something from a nightmare—a mass of shimmering ice wings, all beating, with oddly shaped, deformed arms formed of birds, four of them, stretching out at strange angles and differing lengths. Sunlight formed rainbows as it arced off the Lovecraftian nightmare beast, formed of the half-melted bodies of the ice birds.

For the dino's part, it looked almost scared—something new and unexpected—at the thing it had wrought. It took a hesitant step away from the edge as the new monstrosity made it into the air above the rift its constituent parts had dwelt in, still screaming bloody murder in hundreds of voices.

"Shouldn't have used fire, bud," I laughed to myself.

The bird monster had no compunctions at all, though, and without a moment of hesitation swung with one of the many arms, the first blow taking the dino off its feet and tossing it easily fifty feet through the air.

"Should we?" Chien asked as the two began to go at each other, fireballs and blood mixing with angry beatings and a rain of ice.

"Absolutely not," I replied. "We should get well back from this, or do you think you could survive getting between that?" As I spoke, a fireball broke against a limb, and it continued to rake down the side of the dino, ripping away chunks of flesh.

I'd set them up to fight, knowing that the enemy's propensity for fire magic would mix like oil and water with these birds, and I was happy to let them figure out who was better. Personally, I was betting on the bird amalgam, since it didn't seem to be suffering much while its opponent was half-blind, one-armed, and bleeding profusely.

"Also," I added, "I don't want the winner to think about us at all."

CHAPTER 40

WINNING

Chien and I were taking the smart route and getting as far from the ongoing battle as we could, but I couldn't help but look back every now and then.

The bird amalgam was soundly winning, furiously ripping at its hated foe as it sent up a terrible racket. Had the dino been at full strength, or even half strength, things might have been very different. That monster had been going for far too long with serious injuries that hadn't healed in an unfriendly environment, and it was showing. The creature, which had been so potent, so powerful against our own forces, was moving at a fraction of the speed it had before, its spells even beginning to flag.

As for the terrible monster of ice feathers and beaks, it may have had a breaking point on the weird regeneration it possessed, but it hadn't reached that yet, and was showing not a shred of mercy to the invader that had stirred its constituent parts from their normal lives. Instead, it thrashed like an angry weed-whacker spitting bits of itself everywhere.

Nope, I wanted nothing to do with that, nothing at all. The only thing I really wanted at this point was to see who won, so I'd know if we would have more problems in the future. Regardless, I guessed that it would be a long, long time before anyone could safely fly a blimp over this section of land. Enough of the corvids had survived to ensure that.

"Wow, boss, they're really going at it, aren't they?" Chien asked.

"Indeed, though it looks like . . ." There was a massive crash as I spoke. "It's about over."

With a mighty blow, the ice beast had defended its home, sending the dino sprawling to the ground. From that point there was no more fight. Misshapen appendages rose, then fell like an angry drummer doing a solo. Each got more and more red every time I looked back, and eventually they started flinging chunks.

More and more goblets of flesh flew into the boreal winds, offerings of the slain foe to the land itself, staining the pure white world with crimson. The sun glinted brightly off the feathers of the victor, sending multicolored light fractals out across the landscape—a celebration of success against the invader. Even steam was beginning to flow upon the wind, curling like smoke from a funeral pyre.

"That thing seems rightly pissed, boss," Chien observed.

"Wouldn't you be? Those birds were minding their own business when that overgrown lizard came to call. I'm just glad my gamble paid off. I wasn't sure that they'd be able to get that big or take that thing down."

"Not good odds?"

"I was betting on some injuries, maybe the beast falling into the chasm. Even a distraction would have helped."

"**CAW!**" the winner cried, echoing as one through the waste.

"Let's just hope that it remembers that we fed it, and didn't try to hurt it . . ." Chien said.

For its part, the ice creature didn't seem that interested in following us. Unlike the reptiles, the birds in this region didn't seem to go out of their way to wreck everything they could find and kill any creature that so much as looked at them. No, they fiercely defended their home and themselves, but in both of our encounters had seemed perfectly willing to live and let live, unless you pissed them off.

It was my guess that this propensity was why we weren't being chased down like dogs. Sure, some of the birds were flapping in our general direction, but many more seemed to want to go back to their little home, their tons of ice. Disagreements seemed to keep it from doing much of anything, other than dripping red to the ice below.

"Think it'll separate again?" Chien asked as we looked back again to see the creature had finally made a choice and was limping home.

"Honestly, I don't know. I hope so, though. It's innocent in all this."

"Not used to someone calling a blood-covered monstrosity innocent, boss," Chien chuckled.

"Well, think about it. It's no enemy to really anyone, and the thing it killed deserved killing."

"Would've loved it if we'd done the killing."

"Chien, defeating your enemy with your mind is no less efficient than defeating it with your might or your magic. That's what we did today—not some half-baked charge into a creature more powerful than us, but a planned trap. Winning is seldom glorious or noble, but it is what counts."

"I know, just saying."

"We get to go home. Let's take that win and enjoy it." I'd finally slowed to a stop as I spoke, smiling.

He, too, stopped, laughing and grabbing me by the shoulders. We spent a few minutes there, finally done, finally finished with this horrid mission. It was such a relief that all we could do was laugh as the adrenaline left our systems. We'd need to move further away before actually resting, but we could stop and catch our breaths now for the first time in a good long time.

Both of us sat there, weaving small heat spells around ourselves and rubbing our faces. As we did, I pictured what I could do next. Some of the council had been with us, and they were gone now. All the ancients were, too, leaving huge power vacuums, something that we'd need to sort out sooner rather than later.

Someone (not me) would also have to make the traditional trip to tell everyone about who had died. We'd pawn that off on one of the council members, and if they objected, well, they couldn't do anything about it, weakened as they'd be.

First, though, we would tell the Icehome elves that they should move south. There was plenty of room for them now, and no reason for them to limit themselves in this awful place. They'd need help, but that was the least we could do for Neera's people.

"We did it, didn't we? We really won," Chien said.

"Yeah," I confirmed.

"No, you silly boys, *I* won," a voice interrupted, feminine, cold, and full of confidence.

We turned to see her, the matriarch. She was floating there, one arm gone, a leg missing, and her face covered in burns, but no less dangerous for it.

"And I will be having my due."

CHAPTER 41

THE REAL "WINNERS"

"You're alive?!" Chien said, clearly shocked. "How?"

The question was valid. Missing multiple limbs and clearly heavily injured, she hovered there, supported by her magic. It took me a few moments to process what I was seeing, during which I just stared wide-eyed.

"Matriarch," I said, looking at the injured woman in both surprise and alarm and trying to keep both reactions from reaching my voice. "You need a healer urgently."

"I will soon, yes, but I've stopped the worst of the bleeding, so I'll be fine for a while yet."

I didn't believe she knew what she was talking about. Bleeding or no, there would be disease—there would have to be with the open wounds I was seeing here. Even if she'd covered them quickly, even if she had sterilized them as best she could, those were massive burns. Dead cells and exposed layers that were never meant to touch the air were doing so, and festering.

"I'm not worried about the wounds," I said. "I'm worried about disease, Matriarch. We should go now."

"Oh? Together? Even after you left me back at the battle?"

Chien gulped.

"Don't worry, I'm not too cross about that. After all, it would have looked like I died, and I certainly wouldn't have wasted time on any others myself. We'll talk about it, but first, I've my first prize to claim." Her words were cold, hard, almost delusional, like she just didn't care that half her limbs were ripped away.

With a small motion of her one remaining arm she pointed at the corpse of our enemy. The white-scaled reptile moved a bit, body twisting as something came from its chest, ripped away slowly, carefully. I saw the crystal, large and whole, floating up from the ruin of its body.

"I got the other one already, stashed it somewhere safe, so don't worry; we can't have such artifacts going to waste, certainly not now that we've exterminated these vermin."

"Vermin isn't the word I'd use," Chien said, sounding worried at the way she spoke. Her tone was so different from before.

"Perhaps not, but it's the word history will use. I, the victor, and my two aides, destroyed the last of these monsters, ripped them apart. Then I rose to rule the whole of our kind, uniting us into one nation, all grateful at my kind and gentle rule."

I felt a chill, and not from the frozen wind all around us. She was planning on taking over everything, probably by force if she needed to, and nobody was around to stop her now. The other ancients were all dead, save for her, and most of the elders, too. If she tried, people would probably just come to her banner without any fight at all. Everyone knew better than to fight someone when they'd surely die.

"But we killed them?" Chien said, sounding confused, but I could see he wasn't; he was just trying to milk her for information. That was good. That was smart. It was dangerous, but we needed to know just how far down the rabbit hole she'd gone.

"However would you have done that, young man? No, we'll tell everyone the truth, that I did it. I do hope you don't plan on arguing. After all, while you're good, your friend is so much better, easier to control, too . . ."

And there it was—she'd gone all the way down. Sure, she could control me, for a while, but threatening my family? Was she stupid? Was she unaware of how I dealt with that? Honestly, I'd been pretty clear about it in the past, to her face even.

"You know, I think I do remember you doing a lot there . . ."

"Smart boy. Now come, we need to get back to Icehome. Neither of you can fix this mess, and it really does need fixing. You know, my arm itches, even though it's not there; it's driving me absolutely mad."

Before we could say anything else, I felt the magic wrap around me, hauling me up from the ground and into the air behind her. I had to admit that I was a bit jealous. Her flight seemed so effortless, and so much cleaner than mine. Perhaps she had some better ideas than I, or had just practiced that much more. I didn't know, but it irked. *Mad* was also the word I might well use.

"So, you plan to take over everything? I hate to tell you this, but I'm not sure that you've enough people for it."

"I've plenty," she countered. "Did you notice how many of mine came to that battle? Not many, though few were truly ready for such a thing. Ready enough to take over villages and cities, though? They certainly are, and while I've not too many elders, they're all so loyal to me. Unlike you southerners, who threw them out when they got old enough, we don't do that up here, instead embracing them as new members. Personally, I think it's a better plan."

"Hard to argue that," I agreed, both because she could crush me, and because she had a good point.

My mind was spinning, though, trying to find some way out of this. We'd probably need to kill her—that much was obvious—and if she was smart, and she was, she'd be able to keep us from gathering the mana for crystals, as those took some time to make. No, I needed something, some trick I'd not yet employed, something from a different paradigm than we were used to.

Chien was pulled up beside me as we began to very quickly float along over the ice sheets, not at the speed of a plane, but certainly faster than a horse could run. How long would it take us to get to where we were going? I couldn't guess, but as we moved, I saw his hands, moving quickly through weird shapes at his sides, almost like he was trying to keep his balance.

That almost brought a smile to my face, but I abstained, knowing we needed discretion. His fingers flashed through something I'd only half formed to him once, an idea never brought to full completion.

We'd had so many conversations over the years, thousands of subjects covered. At one point I'd suggested converting the language into something like sign. I'd never spoken sign, nor did I have any practice with it. Heck, even my aborted attempts at making letters had been kind of poor, flailing like a child on a project in the back of a classroom, a secret code.

There were, of course, some basic hunting signs and whatnot already, but not quite a full language. What Chien was using now, though, were those early, poor attempts of mine to try and join with me and form a plan, any plan. I smiled as he worked out a couple of ideas, pointing out things he thought we might exploit. It was slow and clunky, but if we could talk, we could plan; and if we could plan, we could win.

CHAPTER 42

A NEW SPELL

Plans began to form in my mind. I needed a weapon—silent, impossibly fast—and now. Poisons had worked in the past, but not now, too slow. If she detected one, she'd crush us out of spite, if nothing else. There were compounds that would kill even an ancient, but none that could do so fast enough. Pure power was out, too, since we were weaker, and with her experience, probably slower—large concentrations would be seen.

So I needed something small, too, small but deadly enough. There were a few contenders—electricity across the heart would kill, but thinking on it, she might have enough time for a reprisal, so no. No, the brain would need to be the target, and it would need to fall instantly, or as near as I could manage. It would also need to be unseen, and something she'd no experience with, a daunting task at the best of times.

I thought of all the sci-fi concepts I could, and all of their seemingly impossible ideas. Some were impractical, or insane. I needed something I could comprehend, not something out of *Star Wars*. Or did I? As a light flashed in my eye, I hit upon the other meaning of those words, uttered by a man in need of defenses against weapons not even I would want to field.

A laser would hit most of those criteria, and those were hardly something beyond my knowledge. It was just light—powerful, focused, exact, and what I needed to a T. I'd have to make sure it had enough umph, but I'd worked with light quite a lot. It was, after all, something all of us used often. So, I'd need to combine it, then, with something else I understood—head, an infrared laser, close range, high power.

"I have an idea," I signed slowly to Chien. "I'll need time."

"You'll have it," he returned.

The time wasn't for the spell, but to search everything that was bouncing around in my mind. I wasn't an expert on lasers. Sure, I'd used a few here and there, along with other optical equipment in classes, but nothing like what I needed. I'd need time to form my ideas and search my memory for everything I could.

An old man I'd known had part of one of the building blocks for the defensive system the U.S. had been building, a massive chunk of synthetic ruby. Neat stuff, and seeing it, I'd looked into how that worked, but it wasn't really applicable here. I discarded it. The physics here and there helped with the idea of the spell I would need, but much of those were focused around media that I wouldn't be using, or power generation I didn't need.

"Matriarch, what exactly are you planning here? Besides moving southward, of course. You see, I'm not sure what you need us to do."

"Whatever you're planning, it won't work, and it will irritate me, so don't," she said, seeing through Chien's attempt immediately. I supposed being in a political position for around a millennium would do that.

"All right, but my question stands," he said, trying to act compliant.

She turned to me, but I was just thinking, not doing yet, so there really wasn't anything to see. I would have to build at some point, and if I wasn't careful, that would be obvious, but it wasn't at the moment.

"Much the same as you're doing now, truly. Believe it or not, I'm quite impressed by the two of you and your people, and I don't want you as enemies. I just think that you need a bit of . . . direction, so as not to cause problems. In time you'll understand, even if you don't now, and in time, I'll give you your freedom back, as you learn."

She was trying to make a compelling argument, but I wasn't buying it. She could claim all kinds of things while reaping all the benefits we made. This would increase her power by leaps and bounds, and let her have a better chance at beating us, should we ever come to blows. That, and the fact that she was more than willing to kidnap us, showed me that this was just an excuse, something she was telling us, and perhaps even herself, to save her conscience. Perhaps in time she would even loosen her hold, but only after she was satisfied we'd never be a threat again. Foolish and prideful.

I didn't have time for that, though. Now I needed to organize my spell ideas more. Quickly, I began to work through exactly what kind of light I would need, trying to piece together bits and bobs bouncing around in my brain that not even I had consciously known. It wasn't the easiest thing in the world.

"You know, you'd probably do better to take a light hand now—leave us as is and reap the growth we want to bring anyway. All the benefit, without even a modicum of animosity on our part. After all, you did help us out a lot. Why would we begrudge you a little help here or there?"

"I could," she said, almost like she was considering it, "but you two are frankly too dangerous to let meander about on your own. Your weapons may be magnificent, but they're too much to trust to ones so young. You'll understand when you're older."

She was sounding more and more like the worst kind of people I'd known in any life—busybodies who wanted to control you to protect you from yourself, and that didn't even understand what you were doing. Actually, thinking of her like a number of politicians helped. I couldn't stand them. I couldn't stand them on Earth, and I had a not-so-light hate for the council of elders, of which I was now a member.

Regardless, though, I'd found all I needed to, or at least all I could without potentially weeks of meditation, and began to form the magic in my mind. I didn't let it into the world yet, instead just thinking about what exactly I wanted. Measurements in nanometers, compared to colors I knew, potencies, and wavelengths, and magnitudes, everything I knew about the behavior of photons and potential problems we might encounter, even how to solve them.

"That's enough for now, boy. I tire of your words," she said to Chien. Apparently, while I'd been focusing, their conversation had continued. "And your companion is—"

Without a word I slammed my spell into the world, pushing every ounce of power I could into it. Care had to be taken to avoid it being pure magic. I'd seen how that could be resisted, but there was a workaround. Rather than just hit her with the spell itself, I had it altering the world that would then hit her instead. The laser wouldn't be magic itself. Instead, it would be made by magic and released. It wasn't the normal formation, where it built up slowly, but almost like a jab at reality, as fast as I could make it. Sure, it would lose power, but I could live with that.

There was no flash of light, no booming sound, nothing like that, as the magic hit the world. There was only a feeling of a pulse in my mana, then the rest of it hit. A noise like a stiff wind sounded, and then everything around us stopped, both Chien and I dropping like stones.

Upon looking up, my assistant immediately looked away, the sound of vomit slapping against the ice clear. I nearly joined him. The smell alone was sickening, so wrong, but it was mixed with something that almost reminded me of meat cooking, which just made it all the worse.

"Justin, what the fuck?" he asked as he looked up again.

"I . . ."

CHAPTER 43

SEEKING SHELTER

Neera was . . . well, it wasn't pretty. Her head had been halfway ruined—boiled or baked would be the best word, or maybe flash-fried. I wasn't quite sure how to describe the exact effect, but it was gruesome. I wasn't sure it had even affected her head when it came down to it, or just super-heated the air around it to such a degree that she'd had no chance, but it didn't really matter. If I wasn't mistaken, the crystal she'd taken from the monster had even reacted, burning her thoroughly.

"Oh, I can't look at that. That's just . . . Was there no . . . cleaner way?" Chien asked, turning from the woman. It was a rather visceral scene, and one that I knew would be haunting me for some time.

"I was in a hurry. Damn, the smell," I replied as I covered my face.

My partner must have not gotten wind of it before because he looked to breathe in and then began to vomit once more until he was only dry heaving. We'd seen death, plenty of it, but we'd also known her, at least a bit, and this was . . . not pretty. We needed to move, too, for the smell of his sick mixing with the rest of it was really not helping in the least.

"All right, we need to move. I want to make it to Icehome by night." I put a hand on his shoulder and we turned. I put forth a fire spell to destroy the corpse, hot enough that it would render the burned body into ash.

I pulled an iron bead from my hair—one of very few—and began shaping it. We needed a heading, a direction to get where we were going, and quick. The spells to form and magnetize it were simplistic, nothing compared to some of the work we'd done, and within a few moments I had a needle. From there I began to hold it in a pocket of dead air, only nullifying the gravity around it to let it float and point north.

Once I knew north, it didn't take long to get a decent heading on which direction Neera had been taking us, and that would have to do. I assumed she knew how to get home, mostly because I didn't have any other option, and we needed a direction. Like it or not, we needed supplies to get home, and somewhere safe to shelter, even briefly.

While I was doing that, Chien was doing something else, and he rejoined me shortly. Something large that our former captor had gathered floated beside him.

"Why?" I asked incredulously.

"Because they'll want it, and we want them to move south. I also feel that we owe them . . . Even if she was an enemy, those people are in deep trouble without their leader."

"I suppose, and it's not like we have anything against the people she's been leading. We can use it for warmth, too. I feel we may need it sooner than later."

Those crystals were more efficient than spells for simple pure conversion to heat. Perhaps I could cook up a magic to rival them, but I hadn't, and they might even be something like perfect or near-perfect efficiency, since they were quite literally solidified magic for making fire.

And that fire would be something that we could really use. The cold, kept at bay by small spells from each of us, was chilling me, even through the magic woven around my body now. I wasn't going to be able to travel as fast as Neera had, nor would Chien. Both of us were weakened, tired, out of it from the long journey and the hard fight. Even the ancient must have been injured and less than she would've been at her prime. After all, underneath the magic and our long lifespans, along with our perfect memories, we were still flesh and bone, still very fragile, very breakable, very fallible.

So, the two of us wrapped ourselves up with what clothes we had on us, and we began to move. Snow crunched underfoot, and the wind howled in our ears as we slowly made our way toward safety. It was painful how long it took us to cover any ground at all. We had no flying ship, nor even the simple sled we'd had the first time we came here, and the missing coats we'd worn at that time were soon becoming a real issue.

We didn't make it far before we had to stop. Only a few hours of walking, and exhaustion was quickly taking its toll. My eyes hurt from the lack of rest during the chase, and as the excitement of the day faded, so, too, did my energy. Chien was a bit better off, even if he was hauling a huge stone along behind us; he had at least gotten better sleep than I. Not that he objected when I pointed to the first rocky outcropping I saw and began moving toward it.

The two of us cut blocks of ice to form our shelter in silence, forming them over what would be a bed of stone. We didn't have anything to sleep on, and normally that would be disastrous, but stone would be better than snow and ice. At least I hoped it would.

"I'll take first watch; you rest," he assured me as we carved out three divots in the rock.

"Thanks," I replied with a nod, sinking into one as he placed the stone between me and where he'd be sleeping.

As I tried to get comfortable, I felt him slipping a tiny stream of magic into the crystal he'd taken, and the thing lit up like a perfect fire, one without smoke or mess. Heat seeped out into the shelter, filling it until it became nice and toasty. It began to suffuse even the rock I was laying on, leaving it warm to the touch and lulling me quickly into my dreams. I'd had my worries, but he'd been right to retrieve it.

It took us two more days of marching across the wasteland before we reached something I could even start to recognize. It was a few of the outcroppings here and there, things we'd seen passing by, that tickled my memory. After days in this frozen wasteland we were ragged, and those small sights spurred us on with vigor.

Some group from Icehome, for one reason or another, spotted us first. Unlike the ones we'd met our first time through this area, they weren't intent on hiding themselves, but rather looked at us coming and made their move. Ten in total, they would have known who should be out here, and where they should be coming from, but they showed no fear of the pair approaching them.

We must have looked ragged and half-dead, and we really were. Our clothes were nothing even vaguely appropriate for the weather and were not in the best condition after all we'd been through. As for ourselves, we'd had poor rest and no food for two days now, only having consumed snow we'd melted ourselves.

"Who are you?" asked their leader as we neared. "And what in all the winds happened to you?"

"We were in a fight, a bad one. I'm Justin, and though it has been some time, I have visited before, as has my friend Chien here. We seek shelter and aid to return home."

"Wait, were you with the group that went to hunt the great monsters? Is the Matriarch with you?" one of them blurted out, clearly excited at the idea of their leader returning.

"We were, and . . ." I wasn't sure where to go with it.

"Is she hurt, does she need a rescue party to go for her?" asked their leader, clearly deeply concerned.

With a sigh I shook my head. The effect was immediate. Faces fell, and worried looks were shared. Our oldest weren't just leaders to most of our kind, but cornerstones of society. Their power kept things working, kept them running, and the loss of one was no small thing. To hear that she was gone sent a wave of emotion through them.

Quickly, they came to our aid, taking our burden and offering food and drink before beginning to lead us back to Icehome. It was more than we deserved after what I'd done, but there was nothing for it. Now, though, I'd have to deal with whatever powers were left behind, not a task I looked forward to in the least.

CHAPTER 44

BREAKING THE NEWS

Everything was all in a tizzy, and every person who had any power at all wanted to know exactly what was going on, with whom, how, and right now. The leader of the small group that had brought us back had tried to keep it quiet, but the fact that we came in bearing a crystal nearly identical to the one that kept their whole city warm was cause enough for rumors to spread like wildfire. The people who lived here had never seen one comparable to their own.

The attempt to sequester us had also backfired spectacularly, and after being shown to a nice, quiet room, it wasn't ten minutes before we could hear raised voices and shouts out in the hall. Anger was clear in the very way they were speaking to each other, mainly indeterminate growling, and it was getting louder and louder.

"Think we'll have to fight? I'm not sure I'm up for another round already," Chien said, frowning.

"Depends on what they know, and how they react. Probably not unless someone is stupid, but people are stupid." That got me a laugh as he leaned back and sipped on the warm water they'd left us. It wasn't the best drink I'd ever had, but it was sure nice to have something to wash down the dried meat.

"Still, these people are okay compared to some of the others. They're not my favorites, but I might have a kid or two running around out here . . ."

"Don't joke, and remember, Chien, how much they train. Unless they changed after meeting us, they're all likely to be far weaker than either of us. Things to keep in mind."

We knew and understood that our training made us stronger. We also knew that the last time we were here most of the people here didn't train at all. They were made content, presumably a ploy by their leader to keep them together and happy. With how they just put their magic into heating their home through crystals, they were all arcane invalids. Elders from this place would be weaker than even older adepts from my own city, and neither of us were anything other than experts when it came to magic.

"I DEMAND ANSWERS!" roared someone out in the hall.

"That sounds bad," Chien observed, not even opening his eyes.

There was more shouting after that outburst, followed by the man who'd led us to this room bursting into the confines.

"Everything okay?" I asked.

"No, every elder in Icehome wants to speak with you, and most of the others, too. They're making a lot of problems."

"What have you told them?" I asked.

"I've been trying to talk to the ones I know best in private, but people keep bursting in. If it doesn't stop, there will be a riot."

"Shit, that's bad," Chien said sagely.

"Very bad," I agreed with a deep nod.

"This is serious, and frankly . . . I don't know what to do," the man admitted, sounding almost like a child. "Neera has always been with us, like a grandmother to everyone here. If ever we felt lost, we could always turn to her, but now . . ."

"Now she's dead," I agreed.

Someone in the hall must have been a physical with some hearing enhancement because there was a shot and everything got very, very quiet.

"That's no good, no good at all. We'll have to talk to everyone. Can we use the heating room? It'll clear everything up as best as we can."

"But the panic . . ."

"Will be worse if we don't. Trust me on this," I said. "It will be best if we control this by simply telling everyone what happened and what comes next."

"What comes next?" the man asked.

"It's up to your people, but there are options, and I'm happy to help with whatever you choose. Can you make the arrangements?"

"I can."

My words and confidence seemed to have calmed him a bit, and he left us.

It was only a couple of hours before we were led to the heating room. It was the largest room in all of Icehome, and with how many people were interested in what we had to say, there really couldn't be anywhere else. The tiers went up and up, lined thick with curious elves. The crystal itself was cooler than normal, though; something we'd seen before, and allowed us to get close without having to devote effort to keeping ourselves from cooking.

Chien and I soon found our way to the very bottom, all eyes in the room locked on us. I recognized one or two faces. There was Imra, a girl who'd flirted with me the last time I'd been here, and another whose name I'd never bothered to learn but whose face I knew. She was giving my assistant a glare that could cut glass, and with how we left last time I didn't wonder why.

However, there were far more elders here than I'd expected. It seemed Neera had held out her forces from the fighting. I counted twenty, mostly younger ones. If they'd been with us . . . No, it wasn't good to think like that. It didn't help.

Once we made it to the very bottom, and had everyone on edge, it was time to rip the band-aid off. There was no point in letting the people here wonder, or be scared any longer than they had to, so I amplified my voice slightly and spoke.

"Matriarch Neera, and all who went with her are dead. Almost everyone on that blighted mission is dead. The ancient of the great trees, Rolan, is dead; the leader of the southern swamps is dead; innumerable elders are dead. They died, but gave us victory over a threat that hung over all our heads for far too long. Their sacrifices led to the threat being fully destroyed."

There was silence, shock, and a few quiet sobs here and there as people began to understand. I gave them time; they'd certainly need it to process this information, but there was more they needed to know.

"The losses in the southern lands are great, greater than you might imagine. Swaths of land are open, now available should any wish to move to settle them. It's rich land, good land, and you will be able to live there with some aid. There is risk—there always is—but you should know that you have that option. As for the crystal we brought with us, the one that resembles the one behind me, it is for you. Use it as you will, for whatever need you think is best."

"Are you sure she's dead? She might have escaped!" someone yelled.

"No, I saw her death myself." I wouldn't tell them I'd caused it, because if I did that I knew I'd not be leaving this place with my head. "I can confirm it completely, as can my aide."

"You want us to leave?" someone accused.

"I care not if you leave or stay. That is your decision, and whatever you decide I will attempt to aid you. However, can you maintain this place without the matriarch? Do you want to? You have the option now to move, and I'm letting you know. There is plenty of space if you want it, if you want to leave the frozen lands, but that is for you to decide."

Stepping down, I turned to the elders that were nearest to me, those who were clearly the strongest here.

"That is all I can offer. I'll remain for a time to answer any questions you may have, but your people need you to lead."

"I-I'll talk to them," one said, stepping forward, clearly unprepared for the mantle he was taking, but he was the only one who stepped forward.

"Very well."

With that, we sat down and endured a long and what seemed unending afternoon. People wanted to pick and pry at everything. I had to give a full rendition of what had happened, replacing the fact that I'd killed her with the statement that she'd been grievously injured and not survived the way home. That was true enough, though. There were questions about the monsters, and how we knew they were dead, and a hundred other things. Hours were spent on the ability of some or all of them to leave, and what the now empty lands were like.

Eventually, though, things began to peter out, and I was grateful that we'd acquired a room to rest in at some point. I did have to give it to them, though. They'd at least had good snacks at their meeting. The people here were accustomed to large numbers lounging around in the heating room feeding mana to their crystal, and so they were perfectly happy to keep the snacks that were normally reserved for people there coming for all of us.

CHAPTER 45

HEADING HOME

It took days for people to figure out what they wanted to do, days that I really didn't want to stay here. I did, though, no matter how much arguing the crusty, grumpy elves were involved in. This was mostly because the elders did agree on one thing—that I wasn't getting the supplies we needed just yet, not while they were still figuring out what they needed for whatever they decided, because of course they did. I really couldn't stand people most of the time, even if I had promised to help them.

While I was sitting off to one corner of Icehome that I'd managed to secure for a makeshift workroom one of the leaders joined me. His name was Pok, an odd name to me, but he had people's respect and was polite, so I couldn't really object to him.

"More questions?" Chien asked from where he was trying to shape one of the bones for our next sled. These were not the materials we normally worked with, and we were missing our own tools sorely.

"No, well yes, but not presently. We've come to . . . sort of a conclusion, a compromise if you will."

"And that is?" I asked as I tried to fit one of the poles into another. We could have used one of their sleds, but I found them cumbersome and didn't like the design.

"Two parts: Those that wish to remain here in Icehome will, and that's a goodly few. Others, however, will travel south and try to find new homes. A lot of people are nervous about leaving, but myself and others know that being here without the matriarch will be . . . very difficult."

"It will clear up space for those staying at least, and if they seal up some of the tunnels, heating the whole structure will be easier. You should help them work on that."

He looked at me like I'd grown a second head. "Why would that help?"

"Air moves and carries heat with it. If it has to go more places, it will cool faster."

It was hard to remember sometimes that a lot of the elves hadn't been exposed to my personal education or any of the ideas that I pushed out. Many didn't understand even the most basic of physics. Sure, they knew many things, many practical applications, but the idea of air movement causing cooling just wasn't known to them, particularly not when it came to structures like this. It wasn't stupidity, but a lack of paradigm change.

"It works sort of like this . . ." As I spoke, I made a small infographic with color coding and some movements with light.

"Your magic is . . . impressive," he mused as I finished my explanation.

"It's something you could easily do; you just need to practice. There's not all that much power behind that particular spell, just a lot of management and visualization. Your people need to learn this as they move. It will help them deal with the different issues in the south."

He looked at me for a few moments, contemplating, then spoke again.

"Will you be staying with us once we leave?"

"I will not. I am returning to my own home, which has lost a few people, but it isn't nearly as open as the central region or far western coast will be. In either of those places, your people should find a completely open area. Though, be aware that the center is probably desolate at the moment."

"Hmm, not sure how we should tackle that one, but best to figure it out before others try to take the territory, I suppose."

"A good way of thinking," I agreed.

He wouldn't have an easy time at first, but if they survived a few years, there'd be a lot waiting for them. Perhaps I should put together a basic primer on agriculture? No, that would be too much interference in their affairs.

It took almost a week of rushing around like chickens with their heads cut off for everyone to figure out where they were going and what they were doing. Supplies were argued over, and I stayed out of it. Families disagreed where they should fall, and I stayed out of it. A huge number of people spent that time arguing over the fact that people weren't adding mana to the heating room; I actually did help with that one.

Once our sled was finished and we'd secured the needed provisions, Chien and I spent time helping to heat Icehome. It wasn't because we cared about that—we really didn't—but rather gaining goodwill from those who remained here, and the fact that we had nothing better to do. Neither of us wanted to waste time, but it was much safer to travel as a group, at least until we reached warmer climates.

There were even a lot of people who went out to get more, or gather all they could before leaving. For example, almost the whole crew that had brought us in had disappeared immediately after our announcement, and hadn't returned yet.

Once all the preparations were done and ready, though, it was time to lead. I would love to have said that I was at the head of the group going out the large door in some cinematic exit, but that would be a lie. There were others more well versed in where we were going, and leaders like Pok who needed to be seen taking charge. So, I settled into the middle of the group, Chien and I happily letting them take point.

Days we spent sailing over pale blue and brilliant white ice, for much of this was glacier. The cold wind was kept at bay by spells and by heavy furs given to us by our traveling companions, with dense, brown and grey hairs that whipped in the wind as we seemed to almost float over the landscape. Magic drew many of the sleds that made up the convoy, but not all. A few had men pulling or pushing them, shoes covered in sharpened antlers that gripped the ice, legs working like turning pistons as they drove their burdens fast across the frozen landscape.

At least our guides were better navigators of this place than Chien and I, and they made the journey far faster than we could have alone. I compared the last time we made this trip to this one, and though we'd been moving faster with just the three of us, our current trip took nowhere near the same amount of time to reach the edge of the cold lands.

We also didn't come out at quite the same place as when we'd first arrived. I remembered the sea of pines and their clouds of pollen, but no, this time we came to a different scene where the plateau ended. Off in the distance to my left I could see green trees stretching out, and even a few that looked coniferous among them, the start of the pine sea; but, to my right, stretched open land, dry looking grass that went all the way to the distant horizon.

Before us rose the mountains that split these two lands, higher even than the plateau we were on, jagged and wild as they cut toward the sky with their points looking like the teeth of a great beast, ready to slam down upon the world. Those mountains held life, though, not burned to a crisp as the grasslands had been, having been hard enough to cross that none of the fiery monsters had bothered trying.

"I think we'll settle somewhere near here," Pok told me, pointing to a spot on the grassland side, still up a bit, but in a little divot. "We won't be too far from our old home, should we wish to hunt the ice again. Many of the men are more comfortable with that than they are with whatever beasts may be down there."

"Best of luck, and if you need advice, send someone to us. You know where Atal is?" I asked.

"We can find it," he said. "Safe travels."

We left the majority of the warm clothes with the others. They needed them more than we would, and then the two of us began our descent. With magic, this was not some long scrabble down cliffs. No, instead we just jumped, using our power to slow ourselves. It wasn't full flight, but rather more like using parachutes and small pushes to keep away from the cliff side.

"Weeeee." I heard Chien laugh beside me, a clear attempt at getting me to smile. It worked.

"Going to practice jumping out of the next blimp?" I replied once he stopped.

"You know, I just might!"

It was a small mote of light in a rather dark time, a little thing to make us just a bit happier than we'd been. We'd seen more death and pain than most men, but for just a few moments, we got to be two silly jokers bouncing through the air like balloons. These were some of the moments that made the bad times bearable.

CHAPTER 46

RUMORS

We skipped Rolan's people intentionally, skirting their borders as we made our way home. Frankly, with the number of elders lost and the fact that Chien and I were both pretty skilled, keeping away from them wasn't that hard at all. Someone would need to tell them about the death of their leader eventually, but it wasn't going to be me.

As we hugged the mountains, I didn't like what we found one bit. It seemed that we'd missed one or two of the monsters as we passed by, with trails of destruction, now long cold, showing where they'd been. Areas that had been burned were not sprouting new growth, as the monsters must have heeded whatever call took them back to gather up and die.

If not for those initial attacks, would things be different? Would we have potentially had more people in that last fight and instead of losing so many, rather come out on top? I didn't know, and knew that while worries about it would bother me for some time, there was nothing I could do. We'd not had enough information, not known what we were truly dealing with.

"We should start a bestiary," I mused to Chien.

"A what?"

"A book where we can keep a list of all the monsters we find and what they do."

"There are too many; it would be huge."

"It'll be huge then. People should be able to know about the things they're going to fight." I was quite resolute about this.

"You're probably right," he admitted. "Not sure how useful such a thing would be, being that even the ancients didn't know much about those monsters, but for lesser ones, I can see the use. If you're going somewhere new, looking up what you might find would certainly be worthwhile."

"Yes, we can begin classifying the beasts we know about already, putting as much detail as we can and then continue from there. Something for everyone to have."

"There's a problem, though," he said with a sigh.

"What's that?"

"There's a lot of monsters that are super rare. Heck, I still see new ones from time to time, even near the city."

"Fair point," I replied. "Still, though, it'll be something."

"Be a nice change of pace, too. I don't know about you, but something a bit more calm and relaxed would be quite welcome."

"When do we ever get that kind of thing?" I asked him.

"Fair point," he replied, mimicking me.

The two of us slowly continued on, even taking short jaunts in the air here and there. That was mana extensive, using a lot of juice for even small jumps, but in certain places it just made more sense. There were plenty of areas where the terrain was unpleasant, and being able to hop over large sections of it without issue was a true boon.

Progress was quicker than I would have expected, but still painfully slow. I missed my balloon—just letting us glide over the surface like the wind, ignoring the up and down, the sharp rocks, the roiling rivers, and winding creeks. We'd been spoiled by it, though a bit of spoiling now and then was good. More would need to be made. I'm sure Jina . . .

Jina was dead, and I'd already forgotten it. Would that persist? Every now and then, I thought about one of the others who'd died, wondering what they'd think or do, but the answer was they couldn't anymore. It shook me deeply. I'd lost people, sure, plenty of them, but many had been separated from me for some time when they'd died. Having been away from my parents for so long made me not think of them as much. I still loved them, but I'd acclimated. Jina, on the other hand, had been a fixture in this nation for so long; not to mention the other elders and few ancients. I got the sad feeling that their deaths would take a long time for me to process fully. With the memories of them so very clear all the time, it would be like they were still here.

Once we were back in Atal's area of influence things sped up significantly. Neither of us were completely familiar with the paths, but not needing to avoid them made things almost fly by. There were even a few places where we ended up taking small rafts or canoes down streams, a happy reprieve for us during our long trip home.

The rumors we heard began to disturb me. On the trails, gossip is exchanged as often as directions and trade goods, and what I heard was grim. We encountered the first trader at midday, resting on a rock along the makeshift road to give us his account.

"No, can't say I saw it, but I know several villages were destroyed," the trader said. "Heard that from an old friend. He passes that way on his route now and again, but when he saw what happened, he fled north as fast as he could."

"Did you happen to hear about what did it?" Chien asked.

"I asked, but he didn't know. Said whatever it was, was big and used fire, but beyond that . . ." He shrugged, willing but unable to answer like we'd hoped.

"Thank you for the information, and you're sure it was to the south of the city?" I asked.

"Southwest from what I hear; my friend fled as far as he felt safe. You think I should go further north for the time being?"

"No, it sounds like the monsters the elders went to hunt. From what I know, the beasts are gone," I assured him.

We were quiet about my status. In the city it would be a boon, and when dealing with other settlements, too, but out here on the road it would just attract undo attention. His information worried me, though, as I didn't like hearing about villages to the south being burned. Perhaps there'd been another leak between the mountains somewhere. Even if the beast had returned to its homeland, it still could have done a lot of damage.

My fears were all but confirmed a few days later when we crested a hill and got our first look at the area around Atal. The city stood, but there were bare patches of trees and clear destruction outside the walls. I could see people milling around like ants, but not what had happened.

I leapt into the air, taking flight and pushing my speed, eager to get home and assuage my worries. There was little I could do right now, but I needed to know. Chien was right behind me, eyes mapping everything in our path.

CHAPTER 47

DESTRUCTION AT THE DOORSTEP

Isha

"Are they gone?" I asked the assistant when she returned.

"Yes ma'am; what did they want?"

"Materials and items, immediately and at a discount due to the crisis."

"Why didn't they speak to your husband before he left, then?" she asked, both irritated and slightly surprised.

"Because he would have told them to go away and shut up," I informed her with a snort. He would have been far less polite than that.

"As he should," she said. "He's put enough into this city, and they wait until he's gone for this."

"Yes, I'm sure he'll be thrilled when he returns."

"Did you tell them as much?"

"Oh no, without him or Chien around, we're a bit lower on muscle than I'd like to be. I did tell them that it would have to wait. After everything my husband put into his flying machine, I couldn't possibly get them anything right now. No, they'd need to wait and sit on it."

"It seems coordinated, ma'am," she observed.

"It is. They're hoping either Justin won't be able to do anything about it when he returns, or he won't at all. Bastards. I'd hate to be them when my husband gets back. Until then, though . . . have our guards increase the security around the compound. I don't think they'll try anything, but . . ."

"Better safe than sorry?" she asked, quoting my husband.

"Yes. If anyone needs me, I'll be in the workshop."

This was something new for me, not a task I normally took up, so she gave me a questioning look. She'd have to wait. They all would. My discovery wasn't ready yet.

Justin, bless him, had been trying to make a nonliving thing think; to use magic, one had to. However, he didn't understand his issue, not properly. Sure, dead things might channel magic, or be magic, or effect the magic around them, but they couldn't *use* magic. Using magic was something only living things did. No, his approach would never work.

He'd given me notes and books, and explanations, but much of it was still a bit beyond me. I understood what he was building was a mass of on-and-off switches, that when combined could do wonderful things. I even understood some of the basic things he was trying to do with it, and it did work, when it had power.

Oh, when it had power the things he managed were art. Years and years he'd spent on this, going through iteration after iteration, looking for problems, working out exactly what he wanted each thing to do. Did he even see the depth of it? No, I wagered he didn't yet, but he had the time to, and I'd have to talk to him about it. He'd told me of his dream, of a place where we could live safely, happily; and it was possible, and so close.

I'd hardly even sat down to start working before the alarms started going off. There were bells down here for just this purpose, and all of them were ringing one after another. I jumped from my seat, running for the door and back to the main part of the building, and then I ran smack into the woman I'd been conversing with earlier, panic clear on her face.

"Did they do something?" I asked coldly.

"No, reports of some monster heading toward the city fast!"

I rushed to the rooftop. We were higher than anyone else in the city, with a view well out beyond the wall. It was a relief to see others on their roofs.

"What's happening?" I asked around, finding one of our guards, a man named Poken, looking through one of Justin's inventions.

The tube had carefully made glass lenses in it, angled just the right way to make what you saw through it appear much larger than you'd normally see. Neither Justin nor Chien normally bothered with it, but the guard didn't have their ability, so he used what he could.

What I saw without Justin's invention, though, was a black cloud rising from the forest. It was still a ways out, but it was moving this way and fast. I could see people fleeing back along the streets, though sadly I didn't have a view of anyone far away. Were the gatherers making it back? A few streams of color lancing into the sky told me the warnings were going out to them, but would they have time?

“I think it’s one of the fire beasts,” Poken said, using the name that had become popular among some circles in the city.

“One or many?” I asked.

“I think just one, but I can’t even see it yet. The smoke is so thick. Should we send out men to support the fight?”

“All of our families are at the compound, right?” I asked.

“Most of them are,” Poken replied.

“Send people out to get the ones who aren’t. Also, get whatever you have from the armory up here quick as you can. We don’t have the weapons to oppose a beast like that right now, but with our defenses, we should be able to hold it off.”

“Right, what about the rest of the city, though?”

“There are still members of the council around. They should be able to handle it . . . If that beast makes it through the wall, though, we let people into the compound. Wouldn’t be right to leave them to those things.” I hesitated to allow it, to put our families and friends at risk, but I couldn’t bear the thought of children burning on our doorstep, either. “We protect who we can.”

“Right, then.” Poken began to give orders to the others.

We really didn’t have much in the way of heavy weaponry, just a few ballistae from the workrooms, not even the armory. They’d been ordered by a village further afield, but not yet delivered. None of them were even the size of the ones on the city walls, but we’d make do.

Even as they were put in place, the beast reached the wall, and the battle began. We hung back, waiting, sweating, as the magic the city could spare was hurled at it in waves, along with spears, arrows, bolts, stones, and everything else that could be brought to bear on short notice. It wasn't going well at all, even though the creature had come alone.

"How strong are these things?" I whispered.

"I don't want to find out," Poken said beside me. "Ma'am, you should get with the women and children down below."

I bristled at the suggestion. "Go and hide? We don't have anywhere near enough combat mages."

"No, we don't, but you're not one of them. The boss will also lose his mind if anything should happen to you, and the men here know it. You're a distraction." It hurt to hear, but it hurt more for how true it was. "And, anyway, my daughter's down there, and I'd feel better if I knew someone strong was with her. So please, Miss Isha, it'll help."

The suggestion made me want to scream at him. A good leader should be with their troops, should show by example what was expected, should do what was best for them . . . but what was best for them wasn't me here, was it? No, a good leader should know to trust their subordinates, too, to listen when they're told things that they don't want to hear. He was right. I wasn't combat trained, and the combat magic I did have wasn't particularly good.

"All right, Poken, I'll go keep them safe. Just make sure to come back to your daughter for me, okay?"

"That's the plan. Thank you."

I gave him a pat on the arm and turned, heading for the stairs just as the top of the wall began to crumble. Claws ripped and tore at the old construction of stone and mortar, scraping and screaming as they raked across the hard surface.

CHAPTER 48

THE RETURN

The ground was much as I had expected as I sped along over it. I knew that my rush was impotent, that no matter what had happened, it had to have happened weeks ago, but that didn't change anything for me. No, I pushed as fast as I could to the wall, and what I saw did not please me in the slightest.

It looked like the monster had rushed it. It should never, ever have gotten this close, and once I'd checked on everyone, we'd need to look into that promptly. The city needed defenses like it never had. My family lived here, and I wasn't going to let such threats idly wander in while I was away.

"Must have gotten in," Chien observed as we got closer.

"Yes, made it through the wall," I said through gritted teeth.

"But not far, and not near the workshop," he said, trying to calm me.

"Our wall needs cannons."

"Agreed. Let's go home and make sure everyone's all right first."

"If my girls are harmed, and if I find out those fops we left here didn't defend them . . ."

"I'll be with you, but let's see first." His was the voice of reason, the voice of peace, but I didn't doubt him for a moment.

People pointed as I sailed over the city, ignoring the ruckus I was causing below. There was a reason people didn't do this often, as the many enhanced people below would quickly pick them out. It wasn't legal, per se. I was sure someone would complain. There was even someone following us down below.

My home was fully intact when I landed—the best sign I'd seen all day. There was no appearance of damage, or anything to indicate the destruction had made it this far. However, there were things that bothered me.

First was the clear fortification—the gates were closed and locked, and there were armed men and women watching the entrances with hard faces. I recognized all of them, but knew better than to land inside the gate, instead coming to rest just on the edge of my property. There were grimaces for only a minute, which quickly morphed into smiles and looks of relief from my staff.

What bothered me more was the man who came to a rest before me as I made the last few feet down. He was dressed in a guard's uniform and looked quite unhappy himself.

"Justin! I bear word that the council wishes to speak with you immediately. You're to come with me and . . ."

"Move." That was the only word he received from me at his demand, and it was harsh, cold, and angry. This man was in my way, and I cared not at all for the council's opinions at the moment.

"You may not understand this, having been away, but while you were gone, your wife has been—"

"Doing everything she has with my full support. Now move, or be moved."

"I'd listen if I were you," Chien told the man, and I could feel his magic. "Neither of us is in a good mood at the moment."

The blatant hostility rolling off him was so incongruous with his normal manner that it shocked me. Then I remembered that he had been with me since pretty much the beginning, closer than a brother, and almost a son. It was gratifying, knowing that whatever awaited me he'd have my back.

Even more was the men behind this guard. My people, who'd taken shelter in my home were bristling at the poor fool who'd gotten in my way, and I could see them preparing weapons and spells. They weren't attacking yet, but had been stirred up like a hive and were ready to strike at the first sign of trouble.

Did he matter at all, though? Few of the council members were left, and the ones that were, were the weakest. They'd been the ones not strong enough to go with me to fight, the ones who weren't combatants. Perhaps they were depending on the threat of their fellows returning and keeping order if needed, but that wasn't going to happen, because they were all dead.

Tired of waiting, I brushed the guard aside with a lazy wave of my hand. Not hard enough to kill him, but hard enough to toss him a good twenty or so feet. I was tired of people not heeding my warnings, and once I'd seen what was going on, there were going to be some changes.

"How dare you!" the guard roared, and lunged.

Before he hit my shield, though, he hit Chien's and came to a dead stop. This man wasn't particularly powerful by any means, and we'd had time to prepare.

"If I see you again, I will kill you," my assistant said. "So I suggest running and never looking back."

His eyes went wide before Chien, his piece said, flung the man like a baseball going for the bleachers. I'd held back, but he was having none of it. If the man couldn't listen, he'd suffer for it. Would he survive the fall? Eh, maybe. Physical magic users were pretty tough, even the weaker ones, but if he ignored Chien and got killed for it? Well, *I* wouldn't care.

We advanced, and nobody else tried to get in the way.

"What's the status, and where are Isha and Adia?" I asked one of my people.

"Lots of problems, and they should be here any moment. Sent a boy running for them when we saw you coming in," he told me. I must have missed the interaction, busy as I was.

"Daddy!" I saw my daughter from across the nearby room. Isha had picked her up and was hurrying in our direction.

"Thank goodness you're okay! Is everyone back now?" my wife asked, clearly worried.

"Yes, we're both back."

She hitched, and I felt the eyes of the nearby employees shift to me.

"And the others?" A lot of our council had come with us.

I just shook my head. "Things did not go to plan. We won, but we're it. Now, what happened here?"

Before I could get answers, though, my longtime friend stepped forward.

"Hey, Adia," Chien said, reaching out for her. "Your mom and dad have some grown-up stuff to talk about. Why don't you and I go get some snacks? I haven't had anything sweet in way too long."

I watched them, glad that he'd been thinking of keeping at least some of the details from her. I'd fill him in later, of course.

"Need to thank him later, but anyway, what happened?"

"You saw the wall, I'm guessing?" Isha asked. "Sit and I'll explain."

CHAPTER 49

ANGRY JUSTIN

As Isha went on with her story I was apoplectic. It seemed I was going to have to knock some heads. I go to try and stop monsters from ravaging the known world, and they have the sheer gall to give her trouble? No, that was going to change.

"And what happened after the attack, dear?" I asked her, my voice cool and smooth as silk. "Did they come to personally bother you?"

"No, they sent guards to 'seize resources to help with the rebuilding effort' or some nonsense."

"Oh, did they really, now? Well, seems I'm going to need to have a talk with them."

"A talk, boss?" Chien chimed in from the side.

"Or something, a talk or something." Violence. It was going to be violence. "Did they take anything?"

"No, the staff sent their people packing. I was worried one of the council members would come here personally, but they haven't yet," she said.

"Well, we'll have to make sure they don't, now won't we? Please stay here just a bit longer, love, while I handle this." As I moved through my compound I started making notes. I really owed some of my people and would need to repay them somehow. Maybe I'd ask them what kind of reward would be best; that might work.

Chien joined me. "You planning on killing them all boss?"

"I think we should be ready to, depending on what we find, but let's not be too hasty yet. More exiles are sure to come, though," I said as I made it to my personal workshop to gather things.

"Something in the safe we need?" he asked.

"Something I should have taken with us on our trip, but am glad I didn't." I opened my safe, pulling forth the hammer I'd made when I'd first gained a white hair. That was such a short time ago, but seemed so very long past.

"Um, boss?" Chien asked, well aware of what this could do.

"Symbols are important, Chien, and if I'm to have one, this should be it. The tool for building civilization, and for smashing the heads of those who deserve it."

We also grabbed armor for the confrontation. It would do little against other wizards, but it looked cool and would decidedly send a message. We were done playing nice—I was done playing nice. If they wanted to pull this kind of crap while I was away, they were going to see how I felt about it when I got back.

As we ascended back to the main floor, several of the staff saw us and smiled. I'd chosen these people because they were trustworthy and worthy of learning what I could teach, and even as I walked Chien picked a few to join us. Numbers would help, more so if we looked like we were coming with a military force.

As one, we set out toward the meeting place, this time not as a parade but as a force of nature. Streets didn't cheer; they cleared before us. People didn't clap; they moved into their homes. It was never a good thing when elders clashed, and everyone knew it.

When we arrived, there were only a couple of guards.

"Please lower your weapons," one called forth. "We don't want to fight."

"You really should have thought of that before. No, you lower your weapons, and you will get to see the sun rise again," I told him, locking my eyes on the nominal leader of this little group.

"We have a duty to—" He stopped as one of his people threw a spear to the ground in surrender, then another, a third. None of them wanted this fight, and as he watched them give up, he shrank. "Well, I suppose my people chose for me." With a sigh he tossed his own down in surrender.

"Smart man. Secure them while we go in," I told everyone.

No others tried to even slow me down. There were a few people responsible for paperwork here and there, but they saw me coming and got well out of my way, holding up hands to show they meant no trouble. In seconds I was in the main room for the council meetings, and I threw the door open.

Below me were all the seats, arranged as they'd always been, all empty.

At the very bottom, with papers ranging along several of the tables was one of the senior administrative staff, flipping through documents as they were brought to him and handing out orders as fast as he could.

"You there," I called down to him, not even bothering with his name. "Where is everyone? They should be here if this is such a disaster that you accosted my wife. Tell me, where are they?"

"Councilor Justin! It's so good to see you back, and all in one piece. Where are the others? Are they to be back soon?"

"Answer my question," I growled, flexing my aura. I didn't know if he could see it or not, but it made me feel better.

"Well, there's a few things we should discuss . . ."

I tired of his rambling and wrapped him in chains of force before dragging him in front of me. This was something an elder could have easily resisted, but he didn't. He could hardly struggle in them.

"My question, answer it."

He mumbled something, something I couldn't hear.

"What?"

"They're dead," he finally stammered out.

What?

"What?"

CHAPTER 50

TAKING THE REINS

"They're all dead?" I asked.

"Yes," the little man squeaked while looking around as others backed off from him.

"All of them?"

"Yes!"

"And somewhere, in that empty sphere you call your head you thought it would be wise to irritate my wife?" I asked, letting my voice slip into a low growl.

"We needed resources, and she had them; she was the best chance to get them quickly, and . . ."

"And what!?" I roared.

"And I was hoping she'd leave so we wouldn't have to deal with another elder," he said, sounding like he knew it was a death sentence, but not caring.

"What? Certainly you knew I was coming back."

"Almost all of them thought you would die. They hated you, you know that right?" he asked.

"I suspected it, yes."

"It's why the council was trying to get you out of the city so much. It's why they didn't want you near; they were hoping you'd die from . . . something, or just go somewhere else and not bother them. Years, they were planning for years to try and find some way of dealing with you, but then you became an elder earlier than anyone thought possible."

"And you planned to continue with their plan?" I questioned, looking at him darkly. We both understood where this was going.

"You're too powerful, too strong to exist, a monster worse than any of them," he spat, finally being honest.

"Well, I thank you for your honesty. Now, if you'll excuse me, I have messes to clean up."

I released him, and for a moment he looked at me stunned, then I hit him with one of the most powerful blasts of fire I could manage. There were times when I tried, really tried to be kind to people, to give them more chances than they deserved. This man, however, was a problem, and could continue to be a problem. I saw no reason at all to continue to let someone who'd threatened my family and outright hated me to continue living. In that moment I made my decision; it was obvious what I needed to do.

With a deep sigh I straightened myself out, refocusing on the things at hand.

"If any of you object to my rule," I told the assembled aides and assistants, "make it known now, and you will have time to gather your things, your people, and a small stipend from me. You will be allowed to leave this city in peace. Do this, and you will find no enmity from me or mine. Do it now and you will find that I am a generous and decent man. Wait and betray me, though, and you will end up like this one."

My hammer crackled in my hand. It felt electric, wild, ready, like a dog chomping at the bit for what was to come. Perhaps that was all my imagination, as it was an inanimate object, but it was also my magic responding to me. I shouldn't have been at all surprised, but I was; my emotions were tinging my power, just a little.

There was silence for a few long moments, then a woman nearby spoke up.

"You won't hurt us?" she asked, seemingly afraid.

"Not if you speak now."

"I wish to leave," she admitted, looking at her feet.

"Then gather your things, and those who wish to come with you. You have three days. On the third, come to my home and you will be given supplies; then you will get out of my city."

"I understand." With nothing further to say she turned and fled the hall.

After her, three more left, given the same instructions. I wouldn't hold it against them, nor would I pursue them. There would always be people who didn't like me, and now was the time to show mercy. These folks, at least to my knowledge, hadn't done me any harm, or any that couldn't be forgiven yet. If they were willing to forswear their issues with me, I could let them be.

"Now, we have work to do. Bring me everything," I told those who were left.

Things went surprisingly well for the next few hours. I knew, basically, what my people could do and what we could fix quickly. With nobody else getting in the way I could just put through orders quickly, organize things so that they'd not be fighting each other every step of the way. There were still hitches, people who had needs that didn't fit what I wanted or needed, but those were all problems that could be dealt with after the emergency issues were resolved.

Getting the wall fixed to keep out monsters and making sure people weren't starving were the immediate issues. I didn't know what all had happened while I was away, so trying to get answers was important. Many of the gathering teams were afraid after the disaster, and they needed to be reassured, helped to go back out safely and begin their work again.

Sadly, that wasn't the only problem. Merchants were having lots of trouble. With trade routes broken and a lot of important people dead, there was chaos everywhere. It would take time to settle, but time we had. We just needed to tackle what would be bad right now, and we could deal with what came after later.

By the time it was finally time to rest, I was tired, hours spent directing and redirecting things. Chien had even ended up going to look into some of the more vital issues personally, which was well appreciated. The sun had sunk far below the horizon, our last few hours of work being done by mage-light.

"Do we call you elder now?" Chien asked, emphasizing the word. "There will be others, though."

"We'll think of something, and when they start to arrive, we'll put them to work."

“Not going to reform the council?” he asked with a smile.

“Not as it was. It was a gaggle of idiots who could never agree on anything. We’ll need a few structures, but we need someone to lead, someone to get this herd of deer moving in the right direction. I’ll need help, though.”

“You don’t even have to ask, boss,” he assured me. “I learned a long time ago that following you was a path to success.”

I frowned at that. “Make sure to tell me if you think I’m doing something wrong, though, Chien. I’m far from perfect.”

“Of course. Have I ever failed to?” At his question I began to think back, looking through my memories one by one. Eventually, I gave up, too tired to bother with it further.

“Eh, maybe not, but still.”

He just slapped my back. “Glad to see you finally took the place you were meant for.”

CHAPTER 51

WHAT MOTHERS DO

Eventually, my work began to abate, delegated to others who could handle things for a bit, and I got a chance to finally return home. That was great, since I had plenty there to do, too. I'd barely seen my family after being away, and I hated to have to wait, but I'd also needed to set things up so they would be safe later.

"Finally done?" Isha asked as I came through the door into our rooms, Adia asleep beside her.

"No, not nearly, but I can step back for a bit. A few trusted people are working on things, and Chien is out there fixing more things. It will take weeks to sort all this out, I fear."

"Oh, planning to run off again?" I could tell from her tone that she still wasn't pleased about that.

"I am sorry about breaking my word, love, but . . . No, it was wrong. It worked out, but I hated it and I'm sorry."

"Hmm, well I know you needed to do this, and while I'm not happy about it, had you not, those things might have come for our daughter. One of them was enough for me, thank you, and I didn't even get that close."

I kissed her forehead. "I'd count that as a win."

"Should I wake Adia? I'm sure she'd be happy to see you."

"No, let her sleep. We all need it, and I think we'll need it more soon."

"How bad is what's going on at the council house? I heard rumors . . ."

"They're all dead. I'm in charge now," I told her, lying back and closing my eyes.

"Are you sure that's wise? You've already got a lot to do, and you hate politics."

"No," I laughed.

"At least you admit it. Try to pass off what you can to others, though, for me."

"That was a foregone conclusion, Isha; though, I suspect I'll have to handle a lot myself for a while, at least."

"Hmm, well, when you finally get done with it tomorrow, come home. I've a thing or two to show you . . ."

I laughed but agreed to her proposal. After all, I'd missed her, and spending time with her was also very high on my to-do list. Then we curled up together and began to drift off to sleep in each other's arms. It was nice, wonderful to finally be home.

Exhaustion took me quickly, dreams flowing into my mind, as through the night I slept. Others could handle things, though my mind painted pictures of that belief failing again and again. How many times did I see my family in my head that night? I didn't know, but surely it was far too many for any man to suffer.

Jumping from one of the nightmares, I awoke to find someone with her head buried in my belly.

"Good morning, Adia," I grumbled out, not sure if I should be happy or not.

"Good morning!" she cheered. "I've missed you."

"And I you, dear. Shall we get some breakfast?" She agreed and the two of us left Isha there to rest for just a bit longer. I suspected she'd been quite tired too.

The whole way there and the whole way back, Adia told me about what had been going on. Her point of view was so different, less concerned with what people were thinking and more with how it affected her and her friends. She, too, complained that I'd left, causing me to smile, but she wasn't truly angry.

When we returned, the three of us enjoyed a quaint, not so quiet, breakfast. They were telling me everything, and I was pleased to hear it all, smiling and listening to what their concerns were, before I finally had to leave.

Chien and I basically tagged in and out, with him heading off as soon as I approved. They'd managed not to set the city aflame, regardless of what my dreams had been telling me, and were slowly getting things going in the direction they needed to go. It was still a bit of a Herculean task to shift things where I thought they should go, but one that could be chipped at over the course of years.

When I got home, I found my wife waiting for me once more, smiling, happy as she took my hand and led me to my workshop.

"Not quite where I was expecting you to take me, dear," I said as she batted at me lightly with a hand.

"You're not the only one who's been up to things."

"Oh? Something to show me then?" I asked with a bit of playful naughtiness in my voice.

"Yes, and this time something you haven't seen before." That one got me to chuckle, as if I'd ever tire of being around her.

She led me off to the workshop where I had the magical computer research going, the crystals that had adamantly refused to do what I wanted them to, no matter what I tried. She'd taken this up some time ago, but I'd not expected her to actually have something so soon.

As she closed the door behind us, I was stunned, looking at a tiny glowing crystal, almost the size of a postage stamp, floating there, glowing.

"What?" I said, eyes popping. "How?"

"It needed to be alive, so it is sort of alive now," she explained.

"I . . . that's not what I was expecting to see today. How did you make it alive?" I gaped.

"Oh sweety, making life is what mothers do. Don't you know that?"

CHAPTER 52

SURPRISES

My wife was amazing, which I already knew, but she was apparently even more amazing than even I'd suspected. She'd put together something I'd struggled with for ages—a working, functioning, magical computer. There was a slight glow to it, a brilliant thing, a small, living computer.

"You know I love you," I told her.

"You've said as much, yes, a few times." She laughed into her hand.

"How?" I asked, looking deep into the crystal.

"Magic. You get so caught up in facts and numbers and equations, you forget the magic, husband. Sometimes you just need to let it be magic."

"Love, my magic is based on numbers and equations, and facts, lots and lots of facts."

"Your magic is *empowered* by facts, but it is magic. You need to remember that sometimes. Remember the joy of your first spell, of the wonder. Do you remember your first spells?"

"Of course."

"Well, I remember mine, and I remember learning about these powers, about how they moved, and I remember loving them. Not just trying to optimize and strategize and build the perfect thing. Maybe the next thing you make should be . . . something for you, not something for others. Think about it; think about trying that out."

I sat in one of the many chairs in my workroom and pulled her into my lap. The smell of her, the way she talked. She was silent now, quiet while I took in her words and processed them. While I tried to come up with what I wanted, what I could just . . . enjoy. There were responsibilities, and I would take them into myself again tomorrow, but in this moment I would be with her.

I thought back, all the way back to our village, those days when I played with the boys by the stream as our families watched over us. They were some of my best memories, and now I put my magic into them, into the place we'd spent so much time when we were young, the place where I'd practiced magic, and honed it, all those memories flooding back to me in a wave.

And as I did, I let my magic out, let it flow, let it find its way along the paths of memory. My memory was perfect, and with it, I could picture the place in my mind, my consciousness flowing over the land. I saw the rivers that had brought me here, the ones that could take me back. I saw the landscapes, and my mind flowed along them.

Finally, I saw the field, bathed in night, like we were now, and something . . . clicked. I couldn't see it with my eyes, but with my mind, with my senses. I closed my eyes and let it work, let myself touch that place. I wanted to go there, and I felt a stirring in my power.

"Justin, something's—" She didn't finish before I grabbed onto her and yanked.

The workshop was gone. The crystal she'd made, gone. The building, the city, all gone. My chair was also gone, and we fell, fell right to the ground where we rolled into cold water.

"What in the world!" she began to yell.

I laughed. I laughed like a man possessed. My reserves were low, as that had taken a lot out of me, but I laughed regardless. This was wonderful.

"What happened? Where are we?!" she shouted, looking about.

"Don't recognize it?" I asked, chuckling.

Then again, I barely did. The tree line was . . . slightly different. The stream had moved a bit, too, now a bit sharper, deeper in parts. The hills were almost the same, though, the places where they moved up and over still so familiar, and the general layout. Overhead the stars twinkled brilliantly.

"There's no way," she said, head turning about as she tried to piece it together.

"Hahahaha," I cackled like a madman. "I didn't even know I could do this! How wonderful, how perfect!"

I'd sent a threat of mana impossibly far, something I didn't even know I could do, that I'd never even conceived I could do, and then I let it pull me there. The relationships were so different, so new to me, something I didn't understand in the slightest. It was so odd, and I loved it.

"You take us back right now!" she said, clearly a bit flustered with her soaking clothes. We'd not even gotten out of the stream yet.

"I've got no mana, and I have no clue how I did it in the first place," I said, laughing, still pleased as I could be with this.

She stood up and poked me with her toe as I continued to giggle in the mud. "Well you'd better find some. How did you even do it?"

"I'm not sure. Oh, that's so magnificent. I wonder if anyone else knows how to do this."

"All the really old ones are dead," she pointed out.

"Oh, so they are." That was sobering, and enough to pull me from my laughter. "Well, my love, have no fear," I said, pulling her into a deep, muddy hug. "I'll figure out some way to get us home."

She looked down, down to where I'd gotten filth on the only bits of her that hadn't been soaked. It wasn't unintentional. I could see it in that moment—the narrowed eyes, the clear irritation. She was thinking about letting me have it. She didn't, though. She was far too mature for that.

However, she did kick me in the shin.

CHAPTER 53

✧

ANOTHER RETURN

I spent far too long sitting in that field, trying to get us home, but for the life of me, I couldn't make it work. Isha was getting more and more displeased with me as we waited. She was quite unhappy I'd taken us away from the city without getting someone to at least watch our daughter first. It wasn't like I'd actually planned this trip, but she wasn't consoled by that at all.

She did try not to pester me while we were sitting there, but it was a bit of a lost cause. She was too unhappy, I was too distracted, and the spell I'd used was too new for me to replicate it in any real amount of time. I still had no idea how it worked, which was refreshing, but that meant I couldn't exactly repeat what I'd done.

After an hour or so I gave up, picked her up, and launched us into the sky. I burned through mana like water, speeding us along over the forest below, a small invisible sphere zooming through the night.

"The stars are beautiful," she said after a time.

"Yes, I suppose they are," I replied, looking up. "So bright here, so brilliant, better than in the city."

"Maybe something about civilization takes that away, presses it back."

I knew it was light pollution, of course, which had been getting worse and worse over the years, but why ruin the magic for her? So, I didn't. I smiled, said nothing more, and let her enjoy the beauty of the twinkling sky. After all, it was a beauty I'd never seen back on Earth to this extent.

While above, the sky shone like diamonds, below, the ground seemed to rise and fall like the sea. We were high, and we were going fast, and below us, the trees blurred into one another, looking more like dark peaks and troughs than single standing trees. Ahead still looked like a black forest, though, cool and shadowed with the wind rustling the leaves.

"That is terrifying," she said, nails digging into me as she looked down and saw the ground moving fast.

"You get used to it," I said, calm.

"I don't think I will, but we really do need to get home . . ."

The sun was coming up by the time we finally returned, and I was exhausted. We were also seen coming, and Chien met us on the roof, looking worried.

"Boss, you scared the fire out of us. What happened? We've been looking for you for a few hours now."

"My husband found a new spell, one that he can't yet control," Isha said, not pleased.

"Yes, bit of a magical mishap; nothing to worry about, Chien."

He gave me a skeptical look but said nothing.

"Where is Adia?" Isha asked.

"Still asleep; didn't want to worry her for nothing . . ."

"Thank you for that, at least." She pointed to me. "You, don't do that to me again until you're able to undo it."

"I am sorry, love . . ." I tried.

"Hmm." Yes, she was certainly going to be peeved at me for a while.

Once she left I turned to Chien. "Can you handle things today?" I asked.

"Sure, boss. Gonna try apologizing again?"

"No, I need to sleep. I'm exhausted."

He laughed at that, patting me on the shoulder. "Don't imagine your wife will like that at all," he said.

"No, probably not, but I'm too tired to care much."

She didn't like it. I wasn't sure what it was, but women in almost every world seemed to have something against seeing a man sleep. It had to be ingrained somewhere in the laws of reality. I remembered it from Earth vividly. My mother and girlfriends always waking me up if they saw me napping. Isha may have been less prone to it, but she was mad, so she let me have it.

Eventually, though, it was time for Adia to nap, too, and my child decided that the best place for that was with me. Angry at me or not, my wife wasn't one to wake a napping child, and so I got off a little lighter than I might have otherwise, and I got a few hours of sleep.

I woke up in the middle of the afternoon. I could have gone to continue sorting out the mess that was the current administration, but instead, I left Chien to it. My daughter had weeks of things to tell me, happy that I was finally back, and that was more important to me at the moment.

She went on and on about her day, drinking tea with me. It was an old ritual, but one I had missed while I was away. One day, these little meetings of ours were going to end; I knew that, and I wanted to savor them while I could, and missing them for weeks had made me realize just how good I had it.

One day she would be grown, and what then? Would she still want to come and see her father, tell him about her day over tea, about all the little things that she'd seen and had made her happy or sad. No, probably not, or not as often as she did these days.

Nor would her problems be so simple for me to understand. A broken toy was easy to fix; a broken heart, not so much. I could answer most of her questions, and wanted to, to help her where I could. But, one day, one day they would be something only she could find the answers to. I mourned the coming of that time, the time when I'd no longer be there to fix her small problems or answer her little questions.

So, I would savor it. I would savor the time I got. Even though we didn't age, we still lost time, still missed things. Our children, as well. At some point they'd leave us. Perhaps that was why Isha had wanted me to stop adventuring until Adia was grown. Yes, probably. She'd been wiser than I in that respect.

"Something wrong?" Adia asked, stopping in her endless stream of consciousness as she watched my face.

"No, nothing at all is wrong. I'm just sad I missed so many days with you," I told her.

"Well, Mommy says no more going to chase monsters for now, didn't she?"

"Yes, and you know she's probably right about that."

CHAPTER 54

NEW ELDER

Five years had passed since the deaths of the ancients and most of the elders, and those years had not been good.

"Another one?" I asked as Chien brought me a familiar looking page, a form we'd made after so many reports.

"Yeah, from further south this time," he said.

"How many does that make this year?" I asked.

"Fifteen, that we know of."

Fifteen villages, of the ones we knew about, gone. They'd lost their strongest elders. With our race already floundering after losing three ancients one after another, we'd now lost the villages as well. Without someone who could protect them, those villages couldn't defend against even simpler monsters.

"They want sanctuary, I presume?"

"The eighty that are left."

"Only eighty." I was shocked. "Of how many?"

"Two-hundred and twelve."

"We need to expand the walls," I replied with a shake of my head.

Even beyond the refugees, we were getting others flocking to the city. They sensed how dangerous the wilds were right now, and that, too, was getting worse in some ways. Animals were spreading back outward, populations exploding, and predatory or aggressive ones were finding elven villages undefended, or under-defended against their attacks.

Some places were doing much better. Atal, for example, was doing fine; the population influx was even good. With our walls, better tech than average, and the presence of at least one elder and several comparable casters we were in an excellent position.

My own home village was also thriving, not because it was well situated but because I was sending soldiers to protect it. They weren't told why they were there, but I wanted the area mostly clean of magic monsters, particularly the area around the sealed-off cave. That was one more disaster waiting to happen. The soldiers thought I was nostalgic, and that was enough for most people.

The city, on the other hand, was surging, pressing against the edges and ready to burst. It was only through magic we were able to feed them all, and that food was less than stellar at times. It was also worrying to me, since I didn't know if there would be any long-term effects from that.

"Tell me some of them can make food," I said to Chien.

"Some of them can make food," he replied woodenly.

"Seriously?"

"Well a little, mostly you told me to say it."

"Shit."

"It gets better."

"Please don't."

"Other than their main city, the swamps have collapsed, as far as we can tell. None of our blimps have found a single village yet."

"It was worth looking." We'd agreed to help the few elders there on that account, hoping that someone somewhere was still around.

As I thought of missing and destroyed villages, I looked back on the day we'd learned of my aunt and her husband. They'd been elders, but young ones, and the leader of their village was called off to the war. I'd ignored them for too long, and by the time we went to check on them, there was little left. A few scraps of clothing had remained, which had been the focus for the funeral that I'd missed. It still haunted me.

"Please tell me there's good news," I said. "Just, something, somewhere."

"We've exceeded our estimates when it comes to gathering this week."

"I'll take it; tell the people doing it good job."

"Dad," Adia called, appearing in my doorway. "Mom wants to talk to you."

"What about, dear?" I asked her.

"I don't know; she just looked in the mirror, started paying attention to her hair, and freaked out. Now she wants you."

I moved from the room quickly, my daughter in tow.

"What is it?" she asked curiously.

"Your mother has been expecting her first white hair for a while now."

"So? You have several."

On Earth that would have hurt, but here it was an indictment of my power.

“It means that she’s finally reached the next stage, if it’s true.

“Next stage?”

“Of life. It would mean she’s an elder like I am. It would be a wondrous announcement,” I informed her.

“Okay . . .”

“I know you haven’t known many elders, but it is a big deal.”

I found her in our rooms. She sat before the mirror, a single white strand falling down her head.

“Congratulations,” I said, a truly happy smile on my face.

“We finally made it. Took long enough.”

I moved forward to hug her, bringing Adia with me. She squirmed a bit but seemed to realize this was seriously important. That was good; she could use this memory later.

CHAPTER 55

✧

STORIES FOR ADIA

While most people of Earth would have worried to call their wife an elder, I didn't. It was one of the odd quirks of our people, that age had basically no negative associations beyond a bit of hideboundness to it. Well, that and the fact that older elves tended to be a bit less kind, but that was also powerful people, so . . .

Upon seeing the new, singular white hair, we began to prepare for Isha's big debut. That, too, was a bit of a classic thing, where the new elder would present themselves in public, basically demanding people to either accept them or face the consequences. When I did it, it was a show of force and demand for station. Isha would not have issues, of course, as I now effectively ruled the city.

So, we opened a box. It was a box we'd been putting together for some time.

"Iron, copper, clay, and shell?" Adia asked as we began to pull out the ancient beads. They were still the de facto currency.

"Yes," I told her.

"Most of these are basically worthless, though?" she said, looking at me like I was weird.

Iron beads were now the standard unit of currency, and they were even a rough standard weight. Copper was sometimes used, as were a few other metals for high-cost items. The few bits of gold or silver we had were jealously guarded, and Isha would be getting some of those, too.

"They weren't always," Isha told our daughter. "Believe it or not, shell used to be the normal currency," she explained.

"But . . . they're not worth much beyond being pretty."

"They used to be," I went on, "as were wooden beads, which you almost never see these days, and they were carved in intricate patterns. Now they're only for decoration, but really good wood or crystal beads used to be quite the find."

"Why not use clay, at least, though? You can make much better clay beads than any of those," Adia said, helping put them in her mother's hair.

"Because your father was the one who first created them, and he made them in all the pretty colors," Isha told her.

Adia stopped, blinking and looking at me like I'd grown another head.

"It was when I was young," I explained.

"But, didn't you make the metal, too?"

"I did," I confirmed.

"But those are all so basic . . ." she said, almost stunned.

I had to laugh at my daughter in that moment. There was so much she didn't know, so many things that had so quickly changed that she still looked at the world growing around her like it was just normal. It was wonderful to me, wonderful that she didn't have to think about or grow up with so many of those horrible things from the past.

Like the slaves, or indentured servants, or whatever anyone wanted to call them. I'd banned that as soon as I could, and while there weren't ever many, I'd abolished all of it. People weren't pleased, but people could suck an egg. I was dictator, benevolent or not, and I could do what felt right to me, so I'd banned it.

"Your father and I grew up in a small village," Isha told her.

"I know, you've told me the story."

"Well, I'm telling you again. Back in those days there weren't a lot of the things we have now. Times were hard, and when the cold seasons came, it was bad. It's your father who fixed a lot of that."

"Was it really that different, Dad?" she asked.

"Oh, it was. We'll have to get you to talk to your uncle Chien when you get a chance, ask him to tell you what the city was like in those days. There weren't any sewers; that much is sure."

"Gross."

"It was. Nor were there smiths, or cement, or a lot of other things."

Odd that the three of us had never before had this conversation. She knew that I made a lot of things, a *lot* of things, but we'd never been too explicit about it. We'd never really told her more about our own childhoods than she'd shown great interest in. Why? We could put it off if we wanted, and everyone agreed things were better now.

"So, it was like the people from the south?" she asked.

"What do you know about that?" I replied.

"They're really backward; that's what everyone says. They don't know about a lot of things, and are always so weird, even their tools. A lot of the tools are stone, for goodness sake. Who uses stone for tools?"

While we braided and prepared Isha's hair, we told Adia stories. We told her of our friends, of the hunts, of old Elaya and how she'd run our village. We told her of her grandparents, small things we hadn't shared before. We spoke of the quiet moments, the ones where we'd helped each other as children. Isha even told her of the shadow beasts that had attacked our home, and how we'd fought them.

As we continued on, we worked forward in history, telling Adia of our various adventures and actions. We made sure she knew what we had to say, what the stories were. It was our job to teach her these, even the small ones, so that she could know if she ever needed to for some reason.

"I don't believe you did all that alone," she said to me eventually, pouting.

"No, of course I didn't. Chien joined me for much of it, almost since the beginning. The two of us have been close for so long now it's almost like we were from the same village. You can ask him about some of the stories if you want."

"I will," she assured me.

Fear didn't find me as she made her threat. If anything, Chien would tell her even more about how things had been, and how they were so much better now. He'd been in the city, seen the darker parts. He was a monster of a man in his own right, but still one of us. I never tired of spending a day working with him at a forge or workshop, even if we didn't get to do that as much as we used to.

Before long, my wife was even more lovely than she was on a normal day. Decked out in beads that shone and glittered, and clothes prepared specifically for this occasion. She looked amazing, and she would be the one leading today, the one in the spotlight. I smiled at her, happy with the life we'd made.

CHAPTER 56

ISHA'S PARADE

The announcement was made throughout the city that there was a new elder. I wasn't there for some of it, having to go and take my own traditional place, but I was there for the important parts. I saw her leaving the house, her train in tow, holding a small rod of gold and silver in her hand as she began her march through the street. It was a major thing now, a tradition I'd unintentionally started, even if it had only happened a few times.

New elders marched from their homes to the central ruling palace, where I would meet and greet them. They were vanishingly rare, so it wasn't a large pull on time, and none of them even thought of opposing me, though some did leave the city, founding their own villages nearby. I supported them in this. It was good not to have too many people of your same power level around; it kept fighting down.

I waited as she came to the palace—formerly Atal's palace, formerly the meeting place of the council—making her way slowly up the street. People gathered to watch; they always did. They'd heard about her through runners or through the ongoing parade, and had come to the street to see her. It was a rare sight, something like a parade.

Her feet moved on the stone-paved road, hair jingling with many, many beads that represented our lives. The clothes she'd picked were perfect, too, matching her in ways I never thought they could. I'd seen them before, the many parts of this outfit, but never all at once, and never like this. She practically glowed as she moved closer and closer.

On my belt was one of my many hammers, the symbols I used for our city and my office, a symbol of both building and destruction. It was similar in style to her small rod, it, too, a symbol of her mastery of her own realm. For she was the master of the places she claimed, this ceremony just that, just a public acknowledgment of it.

Slowly, she made her way up the steps to me, and I could see Chien and Adia off to the side, waving. They'd join us later, but for the moment they would hold back. The young man who I'd scooped out of the streets and my growing daughter, the joker and the serious girl. Somehow seeing them here gave me peace, and the way Isha looked at us told me it gave her some, too.

"Glad to see you made it, love," I said as my wife joined me at the top of the steps, turning around.

"Glad to be here," she replied, waving at the crowd.

"Shall we go inside?"

The two of us made our way into the seat of the government, past several of the functionaries, and into the place where I actually did things—an office, one of many, that we used.

"Pah, that was . . ."

"Bit of an overdone show?" I asked.

"Yes, that's probably right, but it felt good. It was almost like coming of age again," she said, laughing.

"So, when should I be expecting you to try to take over some of the functions here, or maybe you'll start a village . . ." Her response to my question was to take a paper from my desk, ball it up, and throw it at me. It bounced off my head and landed perfectly in a nearby waste bin.

"Did you do magic for that?" I asked genuinely surprised.

"No."

"Well, I'm impressed. That was perfect aim, love."

"Are you done?"

"No, but I can hold off for now. Is there anything you want to do?"

"That I wasn't already doing? No, not really. I am happy. I have our daughter, our home, and our whole compound to manage, and believe it or not, I find that enjoyable," she said, tapping the chair's armrests with her fingernails.

A knock came at my door a moment before it opened. "Hope you're decent," Chien called as he came in with Adia.

"Thank you for the privacy," I said through my teeth.

"Of course, boss. Anytime."

"Uncle Chien, we're supposed to wait," Adia grumbled.

"Well at least one of you has manners," Isha said, sighing.

"Actually, we were discussing what we're going to do when you finally get your elder status," I told my erstwhile assistant. "Was leaning toward kicking you out of the city."

"Come now, boss. We both know you'd never do that. Without me who would understand your insane designs?" He didn't even look like he'd considered it.

"Fair, fair, but we really should consider your ascension. It might be a few years but certainly not many more," I told him.

"I'm not doing a parade," he told me bluntly.

"Really?" the rest of us asked as one.

"No, not my style. May celebrate with you guys, but no parade for me."

"You only get one chance at it," Isha chided, like he should consider.

"No, I don't. I can cause a parade anytime I want; I just don't want to," he retorted.

"Can I have a parade?" Adia asked.

"Not right now."

"No."

"Anytime you want," Chien assured her.

I looked at them one more time, my family, for all of them were. How I loved them, how all I wanted was for this to continue forever. And, I was in luck, for we never truly aged.

CHAPTER 57

✧

YOUR MAJESTY

True to his word, Chien did not go for a parade when his time came. He was much quieter, simply staying back, having a small celebration, and getting on with his day. I was, of course, invited, and cleared my schedule for it.

"It's a shame he saw it so early," Isha said, grumbling.

"Yes, Isha, I know I ruined your little plan," Chien said, laughing like a madman.

My wife, looking betrayed, looked at me.

"Not my doing," I assured her.

"It was mine," Adia said, now nearly a woman. "You two planning that for Uncle Chien was wrong, and you both know it."

I laughed; her mother didn't. Our little Adia had gotten quite a sense of what she thought was right and wrong. Isha, for her part, had been planning to ambush our longtime friend with a massive party when she finally saw the first white hair. She'd even convinced me to build her some fast deploying decorations that could be put up in under an hour. A shame that'll never get reused, unless . . .

"What?" Adia asked as I looked at her, hands on her hips like she was the parent.

"No, too long; they'll all be rusted," I mumbled.

"You're planning something, and I'm having none of it." She narrowed her eyes at me, and it was one of the cutest things I'd ever seen.

"Careful, boss. She's got your number." Chien laughed, his voice slightly slurred before joining us.

"Are you drunk?" Adia asked him.

"It's my party, and I shall celebrate how I please, young miss, thank you."

"Please keep it to a limit," I asked.

"When have I ever not?"

"Fair point," I amended.

Of the many things Chien was, he wasn't a drunk. He did drink every now and then, but wasn't one for overdoing it. It was a good thing, too. He was good enough at magic that it could be ruinous if he were casting while under the influence.

There were a number of people here, tons in fact. Most of them were from our workshop, and there was a distinct lack of his many lovers from over the years. That was probably wise. Who knew how they would interpret that.

"You look tense; things that bad?" Isha asked as I stared off into space.

"Bad? No. Complicated, yes," I answered.

"Hm?"

"I've got representatives from three villages asking to join us," I told her.

"How is that complicated?"

"Because they're not on our border, but they're afraid, and there's nowhere for us to add three villages worth of people," I grumbled.

It had been a problem of late, more and more people trying to join our little alliance, having trouble because we were no longer accepting refugees into the city. It wasn't like I begrudged them wanting to come, but there simply wasn't room or food inside the city for them, not without really affecting a lot of others. Compromises had been put forth, aid rendered, places outside the city made, but there was still an influx.

Chien chose that moment to return to my side.

"I keep telling you, boss—you need more land. Stop just letting people come here. They want in our group, they bring their whole village, not just the people."

"I'll consider."

"Good, but for now, come join me. We've got something important to do." He took me by the arm and pulled me away to some game he'd set up, one I'd never seen. It involved sticks, hoops, and fruit that were overripe.

A couple hours later it all settled down, and I found myself sitting atop one of the buildings with him beside me, lying on the warm tiles in the cool night air.

"If this is being an elder, I should've done it sooner," he mumbled.

"It's not; it's mostly dealing with people complaining to you," I told him.

"Boo."

"I'll second that."

"You've got to do something about the newcomers, though; make them accept you as the leader."

"I'm an elder," I said. "That only gets me so far when it comes to power."

"Then invent a new title, oh, inventor," he mocked.

"What?"

"A new title. Make a new title. Stop calling yourself an elder, and call yourself something else, something that will make them respect you."

"What?"

"You need something like . . . old leader, or powerful leader, or . . . I don't know." The title suggestions sounded odd in English, but better in our language. "Something that tells people you're in charge, maybe get some good-looking pieces of clothing or something, and a throne. Atal had a throne; you should have a throne. Nothing says 'I'm in charge' like a throne."

"Like a king?" I asked, though the word didn't have much meaning.

"Whatever that is, I'm sure it's perfect," my slightly drunk friend said, slapping my shoulder. "That's what we'll do. That's the plan, a fancy title will fix it for you."

"What, you going to start calling me 'Your Majesty' or something?" I asked.

"Me? What? No, you'll always be boss to me, boss, but other people . . ."

"That's a terrible idea," I told him. "And you're drunk."

"Maybe."

By the end of the next day, half of my staff was jokingly calling me "Your Majesty" which was impressive. He'd managed to pull that off in a day, while hungover, because he most certainly was. Sadly, other people heard them, and soon others began to join in on the joke.

Within a week, visiting envoys from the villages began to refer to me by the title when they came to meet with me, and I felt my headache get worse. Chien, on the other hand, managed to look proud of himself. I really was going to have to give him a title of his own at some point.

ABOUT THE AUTHOR

Wandering Agent is the North Carolina–based author of the Melody of Mana series as well as other fantasy and isekai stories.

JOIN THE FELLOWSHIP

follow us on our socials

 podiumentertainment.com

 @podiumentertainment

 /podiumentertainment

 @podium_ent

 @podiumentertainment

www.ingramcontent.com/pod-product-compliance
Lightning Source LLC
LaVergne TN
LVHW041150150826
845673LV00001B/125